AF552657

Stay With Me

Stay With Me

Maniza Naqvi

tara press, new delhi

tara-india research press
B-4/22, Safdarjung Enclave
New Delhi – 110 029. India
Ph.: 24694610; Fax : 24618637
contact@indiaresearchpress.com; bahrisons@vsnl.com
www.indiaresearchpress.com

2005 ®© paper cover edition, tara-india research press new delhi.

ISBN : 81-87943-86-6

Cataloging in Publication Data
Maniza Naqvi
Stay With Me
by Maniza Naqvi

1. Fiction. 2. Women 3. Afghan / Afghanistan.
I. Title. II. Author

This is a work of fiction and has no resemblance to any person living or dead.
Recreated under rights from the edition of the SAMA editorial and publishing services, Karachi.

Printed at focus impression, New Delhi-110003

*For the love of those who found and understood it,
cherished it, safeguarded it, whose lives were spent in
search of it, and who lived and died for it.*

Prologue

His hand grabs her throat. His arm pins her chest against the wall. His eyes look straight into hers. She stares into shards of jagged light. Irises on fire. His eyes. Her own begin to tear, as the air is knocked out of her. She thinks he is going to squeeze but he doesn't. He lets go and steps back. His hand reaches for his waist and grabs the bone handle in the sheath at his belt.

She stands very still. She sees the knife.

She sees it in his hand.

She sees his hand move through the air.

She swallows.

The knife flashes, grins, winks.

She sees it catch the light. He is swift.

She marvels at his grace.

She marvels at his calmness.

She marvels at herself.

And she has shut her eyes.

And through her shut eyes, she sees again, the fire, the hand in motion, the knife catch the light and she waits. She sees herself waiting.

No more.

There must be memory of this.

There must be more.

1

'Are the children asleep?' The tone, an apology, nestled in her ear.

'Yes, what did you expect? It's after midnight,' she whispered. He loves her she knows for this, her gentleness, this whispering, so that the children wouldn't wake up, her whispering so that he would not hear the anger settling in her voice, of another night, of a promise not kept. She knows he notices these things, she hasn't mentioned the dinner party they had missed again tonight.

'Sorry love,' he said. 'I'm going to have to go soon, I can see the Colonel, pacing outside on the verandah.'

'Has there been any further news? Have you heard anything? It's so eerie.'

'No nothing more, you know as much as I do. I just got in. If I hear something more, I'll let you know.'

'It was so quiet on the streets today.'

'I know, it feels like a curfew, doesn't it? I think people are just shocked.'

'What do you think is going to happen?'

'Nothing, don't worry, everything is in good hands, I'm sure.'

'When are you going to get home?' she asked.

'I don't know, I just got back from the field and they've told me to hang around here, I may be needed.'

'Not trouble in the city again? Do you think there will be trouble, I mean people are going to get nervous, I hope there isn't trouble,' she protested.

'No, I don't think so,' he replied.

There was a pause, then she said, 'Come home.' Her voice was insistent.

'I can't. Something important is happening, I have to stay.' She could hear the fluttering of a chopper getting louder.

'It's always important,' she replied.

'Sorry. I'll make it up to you.'

'Can't we be transferred to a quiet place?' she said wistfully.

'Then that would mean you'd be there, and I'd be somewhere else, like last time. You want that?'

'Of course not.'

'Then this is it, okay? As quiet as it's going to get for me. Okay?' he repeated.

'Of course,' she whispered.

'Did the plumber come today?'

'Yes, he said, he'll need to open up the entire main line, it's not just our house but other houses on the base as well.'

'Shit!'

'Exactly!' They laughed together.

She can hear a voice in the background, 'Come quickly, it's landing.'

Her husband asked, 'Who is it?'

'The latest guest on the premises,' the Colonel replied.

Her husband shouted to her over the noise of the chopper, 'I want to come home, hope this doesn't take all night.'

The phone died.

She fell asleep. She woke up to him kneeling beside the bed. As he touched her cheek, she turned towards him, eyes still shut and put her arms around him, embracing his head.

'Two days without even telling me where you were,' she murmured half asleep.

'I'm sorry,' he whispered.

'For what?'

'For this.'

'For what?' she repeated.

'You never wanted this.'

'You did, and that's that! We're together!'

'You could have married anyone!'

'I married you, my hero.' They held each other. She fell asleep.

He said, 'I never thought it would be this.'

She sleeps.

2

How?

A yellow dot on a black surface, shoots straight at her. The sound, that sound, hard and loud, kahtak! Kahtak! What was that? What was that sound that kept raging in her ears? A yellow dot on a tiny black ball hits against the tin and board at the front of the court. That sound, that sound blasts off in her ears. A shot. A good shot gone wrong. Fault! Fault!

A shot kept ringing and drilling through her ears. A red-black flood crashes through. Obliterating sound.

There is pain.

She passes out.

And then the light begins again, a dot in the darkness, spreading, looming before her, larger and larger, till it is a huge fluorescent disk hovering above her blinding her with its light. White caps and white masked faces just below the big shining disk of light. Faces, darkened by the light above them, peer down at her.

She cannot see them. The light is behind them.

Doctors?

Do we save the body or remove the limb? The choice before us gentlemen is between saving the body at the cost of losing a limb. Or saving the limb and losing the whole body.

The whole at the cost of the part?

The part at the cost of the whole?

Save both, put the limb, put that part on ice, perhaps for a year or so.

Let's take care not to sacrifice. Let's take care not to sacrifice anything, here. Put it on ice.

The doctors take off their masks. They grin down at her. The portrait to left, flag to the right. Left, right, left. Iced.

She looks past them into the light, it's the eye of a TV camera. She has a speech in her hands.

Flag to the left of her. The portrait to the right.

Left, right, left.

Thud-thud-thud. Crack-crack-crack. Clang-bang-clang.

Wake up. Keep awake! She tells herself. Searing, stinging heat burns her. It's in her face, nose, eyes, teeth, cheek-bones. All these parts, so unnoticed till now. So silent till now. These skirmishes opening fire all over her. She felt their existence, the parts, her existence, hot, gnawing fangs sinking into her. This was all there was of her now. These frothing fissures of shooting heat, endless punctures oozing terror. This was pain. She was pain.

Nails.

Fingers.

Arms.

Chest.

Back.

Spine.

Pelvic bones.

Thighs.

Knees.

Ankles.

All these parts, now screamed in unison they were with her. She must change this. There must be a way out. There must be a way out. There must be a way. She struggles with it, she clenches her teeth. No it will not go. She can't get beyond it. There was no other thought. There must be a way beyond this. A condition beyond this. And this darkness, this blackness, she must get out of here. Out of it. She must get out of here somehow. Out of this thick, dense, nothing state. Ink! That's what it was, ink. Perhaps it was just the ink coloring the air around her, it would clear and she would be in a better place. What ink? What was she thinking of? She must be careful with her thoughts, she must not lose herself. She found that she was telling herself to believe. Believe and have the strength to escape, to leave. To leave this place. But nothing happens. Her parts refuse to respond. She cannot locate them. Her arm? Where is it? She has memory of it. It must be there. It must be connected to her. She can't feel where it is. Move, she says, move. Nothing. Move! Nothing. She waits, she gathers her strength. She orders herself. Lift yourself out of here. You can do it, you can, you're brave, this you can do. She must remain focused. Focused on what? Leave and go where? What was there, where should she go? What was there, before the pain? What was there before this blackness? Was she looking at blackness? Could she see it? Or was this because her eyes were shut? Were her eyes open? There was really no way to tell, she couldn't touch her eyes, she couldn't move her hands, she couldn't move her arms. No way to where she could move them.

Don't think about your arms.

What else was there, if not these?

Think.

There had been a condition before this. There were thoughts before this, there had been a condition before this. What was it? It was not like this always.

What was that?

'Remember it all,' she said out loud to herself. 'Do not lose it!'

Lose what? Remember what?

She waited as though for a response and then, when there was no answer, she heard herself sob. The sound of her weeping filled the silence.

'Remember what?' she called out aloud. 'Remember what?'

And like an echo it called back, 'What?' Silence. Everything was silent. And then she began to recall. She remembered. She remembered. She saw a face. A face. It stayed. Terror painstakingly receded, comfort seeped in. The heat diminished. The face, its image, left no room for the pain.

'Do not forget, do not forget this, do not forget me,' a voice said.

'How can I ever do that?'

'I don't know,' he said.

'I am scared.'

'You have nothing to fear, you are with me,' he whispers.

'I am with you,' she repeats.

She said out loud, 'I must find my way back to you. I must. To live, to live again, to be in that moment. I will not forget.'

His voice cools her, it's lovely. Dance with me.

And the music begins, slowly, and fills her up. Do not forget. He had said to her, his one hand on her heart, his fingers above her right breast, his thumb beneath it, the other hand's index finger raised in front of his face to emphasize the point to her. His brow furrowed, his eyes pleading his point.

'Rise up from this cold floor and slip out,' he urges her.

'How?' she asks. She can't hear an answer.

'How?

'You're asking too much of me,' she says.

'I'll come again.'

'Stay,' she says.

'I cannot.'

'Let me go then.'

'I cannot.'

'Why not?'

'I have orders to respect,' he says.

'Free me.'

'No,' he whispers, simply.

Humza moves towards her and injects her in her arm. 'This will make you feel better.'

'Thank you,' she says.

'It's all I can do. I am a hero.'

3

She needed her glasses, she could not hear without them. It was so dark in this place, she could not see. It was black. Had she been dreaming? Dreaming of questions? How? Why? When? Who?

Of water? Had she been dreaming of water?

Like water. That's how. That's it. Now she knew. Like water.

How?

I don't know.

Why don't you know? You know everything!

I don't know. I don't have words.

How, tell me how?

Now she knew.

Like water, that's how.

Water, like life, like that. Like that.

And now, nothing.

Nothing.

How? How could this be? How could this have happened? How could everything just vanish, be erased? How could only this be left? Nothing.

Nothing, just darkness.

Was this all there ever was? Was this it? It was all, just this?

What was this?

Can't breathe! Can't see!

Darkness. Silence.

4

Her head throbs. Throbs to a sound. There was a piercing, hammering sound. A sound, that sound, hard and loud—kahtak! Kahtak! What was that sound that kept ripping through her ears? Like a shot. A shot? A shot kept ricocheting through her head. There it was again. Kahtak! Kahtak!

What was it?

She began to panic and tried to steady herself. Wake up! She was awake, she knew it. She could feel pain. She could see darkness. She was relieved. She was conscious. But this darkness was like a shroud clinging to her, sticking to her like a second skin, and it was suffocating her.

Think light.

Think of light.

Breathe.

Float.

Think.

Think past this. It was not always this way. It was not always dark. She had memory of the light. She had memory of light.

A lamp's glow. A lamplight, her bedside lamp. Soft, kind, comforting light.

Light that meant that all was well, the day was ending in peace. That kind of light. Light catching the rim of her glasses, light.

Light, a glow of embers from a fire, smoke rising towards heaven.

Light, spotlights on a stage.

Light, flashes of cameras.

Sunlight, through leaves.

Sunlight in her eyes.

Sunlight on water.

Water. Like water. Like that.

She has memory of it. She has memory of light.

I have memory of light.

The lamplight glowing over me.

I remember that.

Light and that night.

That night, you broke into my house. Thief!

Help me! Please help!

Pain. Bone pushing past skin, freeing blood, pain. So much pain.

No one comes to help. There are so many faces and yet no one helps. So many people watch, they are talking to each other. But they won't help.

I remember, I have memory of that. I have memory of the lamplight.

The lamp was on.

The lamplight that betrayed me, was on. That soft lamplight that had signalled that all was well, was on. On me, was the light which lulled me into a sense of security and well-being, it was on me. Just then, as I was beginning to doze off, you broke in and smashed the light.

In the night, that night you broke us.

You broke everything.

What was that? What was that?

Like a shot that sound, what was that?

She hears herself shouting. No one answers. A blueness begins, the black becomes blue. Look! I can swim! The whole length of it underwater! See me swim. Underwater.

Light on water, and she beneath its surface, cutting the darkness. Moving forward, with her will. Down she goes, pushing the water past her body, torpedoing forward. The fluidity of blueness, its beauty, its power. Strong and true, each move forward, strong and true. Strong and true. Blue water, dark blue. It's the rhythm she has created, she moves to it, matching the words to the movement, strong and true, strong and true. Her lungs are beginning to swell, blood throbs in her ears. She keeps moving forward, she keeps moving her arms, she keeps going, mind over matter, mind over matter. She can do it, she can do it. She can hold her breath, all the way through the darkness, the soundlessness, the airlessness. The blueness. The tiles appear in front, she is almost there, nearly there, just there, over there, her arms strain out to touch the wall, and she rises to the surface, gasping, rasping, head bursting, lungs empty, triumphant. She has done it! She has willed it! She looks around her triumphantly. See, I did it. I did it. And there is no one watching, no one there to witness it. But she is present, she is present and she is her witness. No one else needs to be there, she is present. She bears witness. She has triumphed.

Breathe.

5

Just breathe.

Think light.

Light.

Sun.

Sun rises, a flutter, then light on water. A bird takes wing, then another. And another. Flutterings, wings, water, light. So bright, so bright. Khuda Hafiz, Khuda Hafiz.

She tries to move her arms. Mine-fields explode. Flashes of gunfire rise in her vision, pain darts forward and slithers all over, visions rise in her tightly shut eyes, she sees bodies fly, she sees him thrown back from the impact, she feels the pain returning, limbs everywhere. The pain is unforgiving. No, her arms will not lift. She tries to swim. Swim through it, through the red, through the black, through the smoke, through the dark. Strong and true. She holds her breath, she releases it, slowly, slowly. She feels herself rising up, floating towards the surface, but then spears shoot out at her, find her, grab her, drag her down, and pin her to the floor. She lies at the bottom, quiet, quiet, very quiet. The explosions abate, the pain ebbs, and all is quiet, all is quiet, fear has taken control and all is quiet. Not a sound, not a sound, not even a whimper. Shush, shush. There, there. Don't let them find you, play dead. Quiet, quiet. Shush, shush. After the battle, rain falls. Water, water, water. Light rain falls. Gently. Do you understand? How rain, lightly falls? Gentle, light rain. Does it fall at all? A tinkling sound, a child's laughter. Falls, at all! Falls, at all! She feels the cold sweat breaking out over her body. Falling, falling, falling. All. She struggles, she tries to take charge, but slips beyond her own discipline.

A flicker of something, a flicker of light begins.

Light. He lights a light, tips a bullet, and empties its gunpowder, into a line from her to him, strikes a match and touches the flame to it. A streak of gunpowder on a floor, a link from her to him. The flame leaps up, totters, dances, a blue-orange, blazing a trail, towards her, moving from him to her.

Light. He lights a light.

The flame fills her mind. The darkness parts.

A meadow. Green-blue. Black mountains all around. A cool, clear night. A mulberry-apple-cherry-pear tree fire, burns. A white column of smoke rising towards the sky.

'Like a rope to heaven,' she says.

The translator smiles. Translates for the soldier sitting next to her.

He says something.

The translator says, 'He says you are very poetic.'

She replies, '*Spaciba bolshoi.*' She thanks the soldier. The soldier looks at her and says a phrase.

The translator says, 'He is asking you why do you speak in the languages of the enemy.'

'Because most people can understand them.' She waits for the translator to translate. She hears the soldier respond.

The translator says, 'Most people were oppressed by them, those languages.'

She replies, 'But it's reality, more people know Russian and English, than your language.' The translator turns to the soldier. The soldier replies.

It comes to her translated, 'What a great pity.'

'Perhaps,' she nods.

He is saying, 'He will teach you his language, stay here.'

'Tell him, I thank him, his language is beautiful, his land is beautiful, his people are beautiful.' The translator does. She looks towards him, the soldier listens and smiles, he jerks his head towards her as he speaks.

The translator says, 'He says, "So are you, and you are welcome here".'

But she knows that she is unwanted here. She has had word of that. And she knows how guests are honored here, and these are just platitudes for honoring guests. She manages to smile back. She is tired, she has been walking since daybreak, it has taken them twelve hours through mountain passes to reach this valley. Their valley. His valley. Here she will get the story she has come for. Always in search of a good story. Always willing to go where no one else would. They had said they would just drop her and come to pick her up a week later. No problem she had said. She was only worried about one thing. Who was going to do the translation? They had made all the arrangements. There's someone there who speaks perfect English. At first, the office had said she wouldn't be able to pull it off, the fighters would never allow her to enter, then this was confirmed when the fighters had said that she was unacceptable when the office had communicated the gender of the journalist coming to write. And then the fighters had relented, because she was a good writer. They had heard about her. And the story mattered more than the hand that wrote it. They needed to be heard. They needed to be born. She looks around her, humming under her breath. As far as they were concerned a midwife has come. It's a fair deal, they want to be heard, she wants to write. So, they don't like her. She's not crazy about them either! She loves it! This feeling unwanted is her best schtick. That's when she really hums. She looks around her, happily. Humming under her breath. All men, all in battle gear, all fighters. They fit the bill with their long hair and beards. They are dressed in military fatigues. Rebels. Their heads are covered with fidayeen scarves or berets with symbols on them, there is the Kalma embroidered on to their lapels, and they carry Kalashnikovs, they are strapped with spare magazines and grenades. And she is among them. Wait till she tells Jack! A sheep turns slowly on a spitfire. She hates meat, but loves the smell of it roasting. But for now she is under an autumn night sky and the stars seem a stepladder's distance away. And there is music. The men start to stand, she watches them transform, they become creatures of rhythm, swaying to the seduction of the poetry. They dance. Arms outstretched, heads held high and proud, chins up, shoulders thrown back and hips swaying, pelvics thrust forward. Slowly moving, bringing their arms inward over their heads to clap their hands, their feet stamp, keeping time to the rhythm of the music of the drums and tambourines. Stamp, stamp, clap, clap. Lunging forward towards each other, knees bending, torsos twirling and whirling. A man sings. He is singing, '*Rahe man rahe tu.*'

The translator leans towards her. 'Our paths are the same, whatever is my path is your path.'

The soldier turns to her, points to himself then points to her.

'*Rahe tu, rahe man.* This is Hafiz. Do you know him? He is the greatest of poets,' the translator translates.

'Sufi poet,' she replies shyly. She is embarrassed by her shyness.

The translator translates, listens to the soldier's response and says, 'Yes, and we are poets.'

'I thought you were rebels,' she says.

The translator translates.

The soldier throws back his head, his long hair shimmers in the firelight, he laughs. The translator translates his response, 'Is there a difference?'

He continues to laugh at her. He stands up, he stretches his arm out to her and as she takes it, he lifts her up. She totters, he steadies her. Their eyes meet. His are the color of dry mountain grass, with ponds of gold for centers. She looks away into the orange-blue stars rising from the wood fire.

'Dance with me.' And because the translator must, he repeats that which is already understood and underway.

The other men stop and sit down, they watch her. She stands there awkward, self conscious. 'I thought you were Fundamentalists.' She raises her voice so that the translator can hear her.

The translator translates.

He, the soldier, laughs. They all take his queue and laugh. 'My name is Murad,' he says. 'Come dance with me to the poem of the greatest sufi poet and we will celebrate God!'

She stands. He dances. Around her.

Yes, indeed, she'll get a story. This could be the one! Her eyes shine. She laughs with joy. Murad notices her laugh and says something. She turns to the translator. The translator looks on silently.

The light dims, the flame is extinguished, the music disappears and she is left once again in the darkness.

6

She cannot breathe.

She must get out of here. Go, get out of here! Must get out of here! She tried to calm down. Why did this happen? Why was this happening? Why was she here? Perhaps this was just a dream and she would wake up soon. No it couldn't be a dream because she always woke up just when things got very bad in dreams. She had dreamt enough to be comfortable in dreams good or bad. And this time she wasn't waking up, nothing was changing, she was still there in this blackness. Wherever this was. She was scared. Was this the end. Why? No, it couldn't be, there had to be more. Just like this, this was it? Surely it couldn't just be this? She must find a way to change this, she must. She had always managed before, she had always been in control. Change happened because she willed it. Choices, she had them, she made them, she made things happen. She had made things happen. Hadn't she? Now, there was only darkness, utter and complete blackness. And she could not change this. No, that was not so. She had already seen the water, the lamp, the flame, the meadow, the dance. She had remembered these, she must think. She was lying in darkness. But light filled her. It would fill her. She would will it. She would think it. She was thinking. There they were, her thoughts! Must make her thoughts larger than the darkness. Events entered, like fractured light through broken glass. She hears her own voice. She sees images, as though pictures disconnected. So many words pouring into her mind. She is shouting out words.

She is in a classroom. She is a teacher. The students are boys. In uniform. She is lecturing them. There's a blackboard behind her. She is wearing a black gown. 'Legend has it that Alexander as he sailed down the Indus asked the teachers he had taken captive questions.'

Such as?

'What is more powerful, life or death?'

And what was the answer?

'Life is stronger than death, because it supports so many miseries.'

What else?

'How long is it decent for a man to live?'

And the reply?

'Till death appears more desirable than life.'

What a ridiculous answer!

'What great sadness it must have been which drove him, Alexander, Alexey, Sasha, Iskander, Sikander, Sikko, to leave his home in search of himself, in search of escape, to spend his life killing, conquering subjugating, looting for the sake of being adored and being in power, and yet at the end going mad with the lack of love, and dying filled with rage. History and everyone considers him a hero, everyone marvels this lost, wounded wanderer known as

Alexander the Great. Remembered for his conquests and not for his quest. And so you see that was true, each of the answers held meaning for Alexander. The captor had been asking his captives all along to free him and they wouldn't. Alexander, the inquisitor, the captor, who had threatened his captives with death, was in fact asking for his own freedom. The need to ask, the need to ask, don't you see what that said about the questioner? He knew who he was, he knew!'

Nonsense!

Her voice is shrill, she cannot stop, the boys look on at her in shock. They are laughing at her. They are howling with laughter.

Look at her, she's falling apart! She's asking us to ask ourselves! Little girl what role are you playing? Who are you? They keep laughing, louder and louder. Then they stop.

One face shoots out at her.

Shut up! Shut up!

They are shouting at her.

Why are they shouting?

Who is she?

It's not a classroom. They are not

cadets. She looks around her. It's a courtroom, it looks more like a courtroom and she looks like the defense. She wears the black gown of a lawyer.

'It now seems to me that we are stuck in the same episode over and over again,' her voice is shrill and unpleasant. 'We are all responsible when things fall apart. We can't really point fingers at one group or individual, we must all take responsibility when things fall apart. We must hold ourselves responsible, we must ask ourselves, what role did we play or chose not to play. We must ask ourselves what does this do to the future and what does this do to me as a human being. We've learnt this lesson haven't we?'

She cannot see the defendant. There is a judge and there is a jury and there is an audience. They are not cadets. They are judging her. They are in judgement of her.

'We've learnt this lesson haven't we?'

Shut up! Don't try to teach us what to do, behave yourself, or we will teach you how to behave!

She is falling, collapsing, fainting.

7

Too much was asked of her now. An uprising? An escape? From the darkness, from the steel door, from this cold floor, from her body upon it? Because there were only these. Nothing else. But there was, something else, she must remember. She remembered, there was a steel door, she remembered being pushed against it. Cold. Someone had opened a steel door and had pushed her in. Slip out with your breath through the crack beneath the steel door. There must be a crack beneath that door. Find it, make your way out. Outside this room, outside that door, outside that corridor outside this entire building, there are pathways, there are roads, you know them well. You know them well. She tried to remember them. She could not. Outside this, there are avenues and streets and roads that she knew well. Outside this, not just right outside, but outside, somewhere, they exist. She has walked them, she has driven them, she has been driven around on them. She knows, she remembers. There is memory of her waving her arm in the air. She is hailing a cab.

She steps off the curb, raises her arm to hail a cab, a yellow cab veers towards her from the other side of the street, inciting a chorus of abuse and honking of horns from other drivers, and screeches to a halt in front of her. She gets in.

'The traffic's crazy today,' the cabbie says.

'Take Amsterdam! It'll be easier right now,' she suggests.

Amsterdam isn't moving and they sit staring at red. Fire engines up ahead. A fire in the subway. She sees her face reflected on the plastic partition, her face superimposed on the back of the cab driver's head. They talk. He is from Lahore. They talk about back home. She merges into him, she notices her face reflected on the Plexiglas divider between them, her face as though on the back of his head reflected back at her.

He is talking about surviving. He makes about $300 a day. He's put three brothers and one sister through university. All medical students. He came over here to do that. Had to. There were no opportunities back home, not if everyone wanted to study. He is talking about martial law. He is talking about supporting the Republican candidate for the Brooklyn City Council.

'What about you?' she asks. 'What about your studies?'

'This is it now,' he says. 'Someone has to make the sacrifice.' The scene ends. She lies in darkness.

She tries to remember his face, she recalls only hers on Plexiglas, she never did see his. His face she had imagined. But the conversation did happen. She tries to remember, she concentrates, she passes out.

She turns in the courtroom to look at

the defendant, she sees the defendant. A face on the back of a head. A yellow certificate for the New York Metropolitan Transport Authority blurring the features.

She looks out of the cab window. Umbrellas above passersby are turned inside out.

'The buildings turn these avenues into wind tunnels, like mountain passes! The wind levels can be amazing! That's why I didn't want to walk today.' The scene melts away.

It's drizzling too.

Like water. Like that.

Where am I. What is this?

'You see,' she hears herself saying, 'I didn't want to walk today.' Pain comes in to greet her and back into its arms she falls.

8

There is a tunnel. A long dark corridor. With yellow walls. Happy walls. For children walls. And doorways in the walls, leading to rooms. Rooms on either side of the corridor. Children's rooms, beds, and tables, and shelves. Story books, and toys. Played with toys, not on display toys. Broken toys, missing parts toys. And there are women, in the rooms. A woman in each room is making the beds, children's beds, perhaps ten beds per room. They look up from their work as she passes, they straighten up, nod or smile or murmur a greeting to her. She feels a warmth rise in her. There are beds, toys and shoes neatly lined next to each bed. And she is walking down the corridor. These are all here, because she is here, she feels it. She feels it. She keeps walking down the corridor, warmth enveloping her. She is walking down the corridor and towards the doorway leading outside, out into the courtyard, full of sunshine full of children and children's voices. She steps out into the laughter, into the voices, into the children. Into the light. She hears them shouting 'Mother'. Some call out her name. There are heads and arms and legs, and smiles, and teeth. Her eye catches a shirt collar that could be cleaner. She makes note of this. Children race towards her, some call her name, the younger ones call her 'Mother'. She reaches out to embrace them. Tonight she'll make an entry in her daily journal: 'My revolutionaries, my Sikanders, my Siddhartas, my Akbars. My Ahura Mazdas, my Baburs, my burners of temples, overturners of aristocracies; busters of bulging granaries barred to the hungry; my ransackers of looters, overturners of castes, destroyers of orders. You are kings, princes, gods, orphans, all. You are like them, you are gifted children. You are like them, you are wounded soldiers.'

And then the light begins to fade. And the sounds begin to recede and she is fading, they are fading, silence settles in. Slowly, rhythmically the drum beat of pain begins. And methodically, recognizably, familiarly, it comes marching in. Down the corridor comes its sound.

There is a corridor. Only a corridor. No, there is more. There is more. There is more. How could that be, that there was no more. She would remember, she thought, she was all over it only just yesterday, they could not have done this, to her memory, could they? She must struggle. It must be intact. They cannot have taken that from her. Her memory. What must she remember? They had jumbled everything, her head hurt. Thoughts came shooting up, hurting her, hard to sort them, control them. She saw them, she recalled them, they danced in front of her, moved on the black surface in front of her face, teased her, mocked her, laughed at her, laughed with her. She is falling, falling. A spider, it bites her on her thigh, creates a wound. The wound turns into a translucent green plant, the plant flowers and a magenta blossom blooms, she pulls out the plant from its roots. She wakes up in a sweat. That was a dream. That was only a dream. She remembers having dreamt that dream and waking up sweating. Did she dream it now, just now, or was it a long time ago? She cannot remember. And this, what is this? Is this a dream? No, this is not. Cold sweat, it's a signal. And there she goes, she is being pulled down, down, down. Gone under.

She's gone sir!

Wake her up!

Cold, ice, wet, shock, knocks her back to the light.

She shivers. 'Moonlight in Bamiyan.'

What is she going on about?

'A face you defaced on the side of a mountain, whispered peace to me.'

Who?

'Me. But he was wrapped in folds carved of rock. Folds upon folds of folds. He was made of rock. But he was whispering to me, you see, whispering, "Come let me heal these wounds. Ahura Mazda".'

Who?

'Creator of twins. Spenta Mainyu. Angra Mainyu, Ahriman.'

Who?

'Construction and destruction.'

Who?

'Jabbar and Kareem.'

What is she talking about?

'Whispering to me, Rehman and Rahim.'

9

The beauty of the hunt at dawn.

The perfect ethics of a clean shoot.

Painless. To kill without causing pain.

Ethical.

Moral.

A duty.

An obligation.

A noble thing.

A commitment.

A burden.

The boat sways on the lake. The sun's first light hits the water, quivers. The murghabis stir. A fluttering begins.

He has been waiting. A single

murghabi takes flight. Humza rises in the boat, follows the bird's trajectory with the muzzle of his gun, takes aim. Fires.

Then, again.

Again.

Again and again and again and again.

Other boats, other shots.

Sunlight on water, blood drops.

Birds gently fall. Plop, plop, plop, go the falls.

The beauty, the perfection of a hunt at dawn.

10

When she comes to, there is the sound of birds quarreling in the trees. She is in her mother's lawn, they are seated in wicker chairs, she is curled up in hers. She watches her mother pour tea. She watches a leaf twirl its way down to the ground. Sunlight, dips into the edge of the arc, of the tea, as it pours out of the teapot, it creates a new horizon, that she will drink. Its rays flash into her eyes and cause her to squint. The purity of it, this moment. She makes a mental note of it, she would remember this, she would recall it, at some point. She would at the very least repeat it as poetry, for Jack. She'll work with the words about sunlight reflected off tea. She'll think about it. Come up with something really good. Something clever. She smiles inwardly, she would come up with something good, Jack would think so too. They would laugh, he would tease her for her obsession, with tea. He'll reach out to poke her in the ribs, she'll laugh and dodge him. It'll be so cute. They would be a couple, people walking by would smile. Their shared moment. They'll feel good.

'Don't do it,' her mother says.

'It's an honor. Jack says it's an honor,' she replies nonchalantly.

'It's not an honor! Nothing will change. Please don't do it,' her mother's voice is urgent.

'They say they are going to restore democracy, root out corruption.'

'When have they not said this?'
Each time they bring in a civilian face, then that person rebels, doesn't do their bidding and that's that. They've never allowed things to work!'

'I can't think that way, it's much too cynical.' She tries to sound light and optimistic.

'Please, you know better than this, you're being swayed by the moment, the fact that they're asking you. It's a seduction.'

'It is. It is. I can't pass this up. It's my chance to make a difference.' Her voice sounds like she is whining.

'You will never make a difference.'

'No, Mother, only you can make a difference, with all your good deeds!'

'I meant they will never let you.'

'You can't say that. Things are different now. They need me.'

'They don't need you. They like the story you wrote. They think you can serve them well. If you say no, they'll go to the next pretty face.'

'Don't insult me,' she says angrily.

'You insult yourself! Just look at what you wrote!' Her mother too is angry. Very cross. She has stood up.

'C'mon don't be that way, you're my mother, you should be excited.'

'Don't talk to me, I am warning you, Ava, if you do this, I will never ever want to talk to you again. If you do this, if you do this for the sake of accolades, you are not my daughter any more!'

'Everyone can't get their accolades like you. I'm no saint like you. I don't want what you do!' she shouts at her mother. 'I can't be you! I won't run hospices and orphanages. I'm not you.'

Her mother walks away, leaves her alone.

She would recall this moment, for Jack. Because relating to Jack the things that happened to her, was important to her, about the tea and the light through it and this moment. This moment, in which, a new horizon came into view, a poem poured, and her mother disowned her.

11

She is dreaming. Is this a dream, she is dreaming.

'What are little girls made of?'

We miscalculated about you. Just tell us the truth. Just tell us that you betrayed the country. Confess to it. Did you think you could write a speech renouncing us, question our budgets, our borders, our defense policy? Education and health services instead of defense. Sign this confession and we'll put you on the next plane and send you back to your friends.

Please just tell them what they want to hear, please just do as they say.

For godssake, don't do this to us. We are

decent men. We have families. Children, wives, mothers. We don't want to do this. Don't turn us into criminals. We are trying to protect this country. We've lived here all our lives, you only come and go. There are some realities you simply don't understand.

'What are little girls made of?'

You are making it very hard. You are not from here, you haven't lived here long enough to be from here. You were given an honor, you chose to kick us in the face for honoring you. They wanted you to be our representative, show the world that we weren't what they made us out to be. But you betrayed us as well. You simply don't understand. You don't understand the realities here.

'What are little girls made of?'

Did you expect to be able to say what you did publicly and get away with it? Did you really expect that to happen? You can't expect us to open up and let down our guard, the country will disintegrate within days if we do that. There are some things you simply don't know. You haven't seen what I have seen, you haven't understood this land, our lives, the people, the way I have. I love it, I stepped forward to die for it, willingly. Did you? I signed up for that. To die for it willingly. I know this country, every nook and corner, I've shed my blood for it, in its snow and its sands. Please, talk!

'What are little girls made of?'

She is so good. So kind, so generous. So dignified, so poised, so smart, so bright, so accomplished, so intelligent, so sophisticated, so wise, so right, so always right. She passes out.

12

'Skeletons of a woman and a baby, a grave of a mother and child.' She leans forward, he has caught her attention. Jack notices this, he stops talking.

'Yes?' she encourages him. 'Go on.'

He frowns. 'The baby's skeleton is placed between the woman's lower legs, under the calf bone of one leg. What are those bones called?' he asks her, snapping his fingers near his right ear, as though to jog his memory.

She shrugs her shoulders.

'Anyway. The pelvic area looks like a heart, and the end of the spine shows through the pelvic bone, and looks like a heart shape within a heart shape. A valentine's heart that is, not the muscle.' He smiles at her.

Pottery is buried with her. Vessels of many sizes, terracotta. Jack has counted 21, but some could be stones. He can't tell from the slide. Slide no. 72. Grave. Circa 3000 BC. Indus civilization. It's a dig from Mohenjo-Daro, a slide of a dig, that he has downloaded off the web.

'Another group of grave robbers, perhaps in antiquity had been there much before this dig, and of course before me. The arms of the woman were broken…'

She winces. Five thousand years later these injuries hurt her.

'And the caption reads that the woman would have been wearing ornaments such as bangles on her arms which could have been stolen and which explained the broken arm. The fact that a baby was buried with her seemed to indicate their deaths during childbirth,' Jack says.

Five thousand years later Jack has downloaded them. She is amazed by this.

'Abraham was born in Iraq, 1950 BC,

probably 1500 years after her death!' Jack muses.

But she is not thinking about the significance of Abraham's birth so much later than that of the woman and her child. It's the slide that bothers her. The crime, somehow, of it. To be humiliated into perpetuity. Exposed that way, to the entire world to stare at, in curiosity, in disgust, in pity, in apathy, for history? For what? She feels angry with Jack. But she smiles.

'I found another seal. Of a woman, a goddess, a warrior. One side of the tablet shows a person killing a water buffalo with a spear, with one foot pressing the head down and one arm holding the tip of a horn. On the other side of this tablet is a female deity who is fighting two tigers and standing on an elephant. A single Indus script depicting a wheel with spokes is etched above the head of the deity.'

'What do you make of this?' she asks.

'Sacrifice to the gods for immortality.'

'Women were hunters and warriors then?'

'Well certainly the images seemed to show that this was so. She exists, you see,'

Jack tells her passionately. 'She goes on, this woman in the grave, who lived much before Zoroaster, Cyrus, Darius, Buddha, Alexander, Chandragupta, the Mauryas, the Mongols, Mahmud of Ghazni, the Arabs, Babur, the English, your generals, the Taliban. Much before this whole lot!' Amazing, you dig into the earth in this land and look what comes up from just below its surface!'

She gingerly lifts a California roll to her mouth. Five thousand years later, 10,000 miles away from that piece of earth she claims as hers, Jack has dug it up. Jack has downloaded a grave, made distance irrelevant, eradicated time.

They are soul mates, Jack and she, they dig up things. She tells him about the story she's going to follow up on in Afghanistan, told by 40 midwives in 40 interviews, to an anthropologist doing her Ph.D. on women's health.

'So you're done with freedom fighters in the Caucasus and Central Asia, and are moving south I see!'

'Well, I thought this would be less taxing but in the general region! But listen

Jack this is fascinating. These are stories about a special kind of birth, short-lived, at most, lasting a few hours. Children wistfully remembered by the midwives, forever, as special. They say, these children were meant for greatness had they lived. The 40 midwives, all, had repeated, the same idea that this was Alexander reincarnated, the child before burial was always named Sikander. Sikander Zulqarnain—Alexander of the two horns. Why would there be folklore for Alexander?' she asks Jack.

Jack laughs, 'Sikander Zulqarnain wasn't Alexander, darling. Sikander Zulqarnain, was Cyrus the Great, the greatest Persian Emperor, he wore a horned helmet. He is the one that the midwives were probably alluding to as being reincarnated in those babies. He ruled Bactria, present day Afghanistan, much before Alexander was even born.'

'But there is a legend about Alexander being born with horns too!'

'Trust me this is about Cyrus! Even though they probably don't even know this! The Greco-Persian influence is so interwoven. And the horns may not be about Cyrus' helmet, you know horns are everywhere in those seals. You see horns signify virility, power. I downloaded another seal as well, from Mohenjo-Daro, a steatite seal which shows a nude male deity with three faces, seated in a yogic position, feet pressed together into the groin, hands on knees, wearing a horned headdress, he wears seven bangles on his left arm and six on the right.'

'What do you think the bangles represent?'

'Who knows! It is the Indus civilization, perhaps they symbolize the rivers, Indus and its tributaries. Sutlej, Chenab, Ravi, Jhelum, Kabul and Beas. Indus and its six tributaries. So, perhaps, the bangles on his right arm symbolize the Indus as a whole, the land, the region and the six on the left, its tributaries?'

'That's clever of you.'

They fall silent again concentrating on their lunch. Then she asks, 'Do you believe that to tell a story, to write down the names of people, is a way to save their souls?'

'You want to save these children?'

They look at each other. She looks away first.

Candles. Songs. Happy Birthday to You, Happy Birthday to You. Songs. '*Dehka na tha kabhi hum ne ye suma, aisa nasha tere pyar ne kya, kho gai sapnon mey hum, duniya humey ab jo kahey.*' Songs, clapping, cheering, children's faces. There is music and there is dancing. Flickering candles, flames. Dancing men around a fire, holding machine guns above their heads. A happy face of a woman, clapping to their rhythm. Whose face, her face? Who was she? Was that her? How can she have a memory of her own face beyond a mirror? In and out of flames and darkness, red and blackness. Here she comes and here she goes.

She can hear the sound of people cheering, clapping, shouting, she can hear music on loudspeakers, she can see colorful banners, faces, waves upon waves of faces, arms and hands reaching up to her. There are shots being fired, fireworks, batons, tear gas, black smoke, screaming, shouting and shrieking.

Two girls. 'Mommy!'

Red carpeted steps being climbed,

going up to a stage, cheers and clapping, manicured fingers, hands grabbing the award, lights flashing, there are cameras and spotlights.

A woman's face in the spotlight. Diamond earrings, red lips, black mascara, high cheek-bones. She is beautiful. Who is she. Her? Is that her? Her face. Is this me?

'Thank you, thank you, this is truly an honor... This award today means a lot to me... Especially in this gathering of... And so with this, I must conclude... After a lot of soul searching, I'm beginning to come to a broad conclusion that the question of identity is best explained for me not through territory and their boundaries, but through ideas and values which I believe in. Borders are irrelevant between us, militaries are redundant. The best defense is in safeguarding life through health services and education.' Applause. Then the same sentences repeated again. Applause, then again, over and over again. There is clapping, so much clapping, so loud, so loud.

Then the claps turn to slaps. The slaps hit her, hard, she hears them, they sound exactly like the claps, when they are against her cheeks, she notes that against her eardrums they are like cannons being fired, like bombs exploding, like waves crashing, like that.

Like that. The pain missiles through her ear canal. The noise of it drowns her. She cannot stay above it. Down she goes. Down under.

Jack's voice beams down to her from the stars as she accesses her voicemail, from a blue-green meadow, sitting under the night sky, pushing buttons on the satellite phone, while a soldier with a Kalashnikov watches nearby. First, a groan in response to her recorded message, 'Oh no you're gone before I could get to you and you won't be back till early November. Geeeeez !' And she, so far away, thrilled, because it was Jack, perhaps, too, because she was missed. She looks up at the clear night and the stars, one eye on Murad she concentrates on Jack's voice, as it rises and falls, like waves, it has a rhythm, 'I didn't think your leaving would do this me, but there you are.' To her, Jack sounded like he was sad, she thinks it's her imagination. Jack was saying, 'Anyway, it got me thinking about so many things. I want us to do some talking when you get back. Okay?'

She wanted to be missed. Maybe that's why she was out there anyway. For it to register, when she was not there. There. Where was there? That, there that she has always wanted to be in? That, there, she had promised herself, would be. She has memory of it. A memory of a promise? She is confused.

A house, a fireplace, a peach chaise lounge in a yellow room.

Two little girls dancing. Aman and Iman. Yes, Aman and Iman.

She sighs, 'Aman and Iman.' And the pain comes back. A little girl carries a yellow umbrella, falls into the swimming pool, there is thunder. Lightning strikes the umbrella, she watches the little girl. A woman dives in, rescues the little girl. The child is limping on account of the lightning, she is bent over, but slowly she straightens out. All is well, thank God all is well. Was that a dream?

Just a painting. What? Did someone mention a painting?

A painting. Which one?

Faces, of men, women, children.

Faces. A face. Through the mist there is a face.

A man's face. A worried, anxious, preoccupied face. A gaunt, silver-haired, tanned, green-eyed, spectacled, Jack face. She keeps glancing towards Jack's face. She is walking beside him listening to him. A pathway with golden orange leaves, in a meadow surrounded by tall buildings. Jack is looking at her.

'It's an honor,' he is saying.

'Do you think so?'

'Well to be called in to be at the helm.'

'To be the face, you mean,' she laughs.

'To lead, to take charge, to represent,' he says with a flourish of his arm.

'To be a front!'

'But still an honor,' he replies.

'Why me?'

'Why not you?' he throws back.

'Scraping the bottom, aren't they?' she asks nervously, shyly.

'They've tried others, politicians, bankers, businessmen,' he says matter-of-factly.

'And now me?'

'Why not?' he teases her.

'Have to admit, they're smart.'

'They always have been. You seem to have articulated their point,' Jack laughs. His laugh goes on and on and on. And fades away. And the wailing begins.

Wailing, crying, white chaddars, black chaddars, a funeral. Women crowding in the door watching a funeral leaving the house. She watches the women in the doorway as they become smaller and smaller, arms outstretched they are reaching out to her. What was this, was this memory?

Which ones went where?

Which ones happened?

Which ones belonged to the plans she had made?

Which ones belonged to her?

Which ones belonged to others?

Which ones were reality?

Which ones were dreams?

Which ones were realized?

Which ones were left as desires, fears?

All of them were there in her head but what was the difference between what should have been and what was. Did the plans outweigh the reality?

'What can never be taken away from us?' a voice asks.

'Memory,' she replies.

'Imagination,' the voice adds.

'Yes, imagination too,' she agrees.

'But memory can be taken away. Disease can do that,' the voice says.

'Yes. And old age,' she adds.

'Or an accident or torture?' the voice suggests.

'Well, yes,' she concedes.

'But imagination, no one can take that,' the voice says.

'Yes. Perhaps,' she says.

'What will, I wonder, I remember when all else fails. What does one return to, to carry one through?'

'Carry one through?' the voice asks.

'Yes, carry one through pain, inexplicable pain and suffering, what will carry me?'

'Whatever is important.'

'Yes, what is most important? Of all the things that happen in one's life what is most important? But you see, that's the thing, it's unclear that what's important is something that actually happened or is imagined,' she says.

'What?' the voice asks.

'Well if it is imagined, then it too is part of memory and so when all memory fails, then perhaps what stays and what fades will include equal parts of both,' she says.

'The imagined and the realized,' the voice says.

'Yes, the imagined and the realized,' she echoes.

'What stays, is?' the voice asks.

'Yes.'

'What can be recalled was?' the voice asks.

'I think so,' she replies.

She saw a swing, a rope, a tree, a dog, sunshine, dolls.

A wedding song, a house covered with fairy lights, fairy lights in the trees, fairy lights on the boundary walls, a wedding dance, a wedding dress, a wedding ceremony.

What was I?

Who am I?

Who?

13

She heard children's voices laughing, shouting, calling out to each other.

She moves to gaze out of a window. It's a school yard, a playground, children playing in a courtyard. She moves away from the window and walks out of the room, down the corridor. Her limbs are aching. Arthritis is creeping in, the season is changing. She kneads the palms of both her hands. Yoga this morning was painful, so was namaz. Rooms on either side of the corridor, a woman in each room is making the beds, children's beds, perhaps ten per room. There are beds and toys and shoes neatly lined next to each bed. She is walking down the corridor and out into the courtyard full of sunshine, full of children and children's voices. Children race towards her, some call her name, the younger ones call her 'Mother'. She is talking to the children. The chowkidar, who should be at the gate, is coming towards her. He is hurrying towards her. Running towards her. He is trying to signal, say something important, urgent. He looks worried. He is running towards her, waving his arms. He is wearing a face that says I want you to know I'm trying to protect you. Right behind him, there are men, in uniform. She notes they are not the police. One of them is dressed in full uniform, he is in front of the others, right behind the chowkidar. The children turn to look at the approaching men. One child starts to scream in panic.

'They are going to arrest us! They are going to kill us. Help!'

There is fear. She feels fear. She feels the fear of a child go through her. The shaking of a child clinging to her in fear, is making her tremble. Fear transmits fast, she notices. Fear travels quickly. The others are frightened too. Now all the children are crying. She is shushing them, they are huddling up against her. Her legs are shaking. She feels like a hen with all the children gathering into the folds of her clothing, some have made a tent out of her muslin dupatta, she's barely able to hold on to it, with all the commotion.

The man in uniform is grinning. He has a stick under his arm. Like a bandmaster, she notes. He walks up to her, stamps his foot and salutes her. Then he jerks his body forward, thrusts out his hand and clasps her hand and shakes it violently.

Madam. An honor. Your children need you, your country needs you.

'Oh no!' the child cries. 'He is going to arrest mother!'

Women, from the inside, from the corridor and rooms inside, have come running out.

There is a ring of women and children around her. The chowkidar is trying to look protective.

The man in uniform is trying not to grin.

He is talking.

Hour of crisis.

History is in the making.

You must serve.

Duty calls.

Exemplary life.

Beyond rebuke.

Loved by all.

Transparency.

Accountability.

Integrity.

Honesty.

'No, I cannot,' she stammers.

You disappoint me.

He about-turns, to leave.

'But, please, I will not let you leave without at least a glass of water,' she says.

What?

'Water.' She hears her voice receding.

Like water. Like that.

What was that, what was that?

It was 'No, I cannot'. Wasn't it? she asks herself in panic.

After a lifetime, it must have been. Of course, it must have been.

After all, after all, it must have been.

It must have been.

She must have said, 'No, I cannot'.

The cell closes in, swallows her up again, she disappears.

A beautiful woman in a purple sari and a black swing coat bends over, tucks her in, gathers her up with her scent. Her mother, she smelt the scent of *Fidji.*

We'll be home soon.

Will I be asleep?

Yes.

14

Should she wait now, should she stay and wait?

It's so cold, it is so dark. Where is this? Is she in a room? She thinks she is, she remembers entering a room with a steel door. What happened then? She cannot recall. What happened after she entered? What happened when she left? In spiked cleats, pain edges forward. She passes out.

'What's wrong with it?' someone asks.

'I don't know, it just froze on me,' she says.

'Let's check the hard drive.'

'Do you think I've lost my files,' she asks anxiously.

'We'll see.'

'I can't lose my files,' she says.

'We'll see, don't panic.'

'I can't lose the story,' she says.

'You won't, relax.'

'I can't lose it!' She panics. She is shouting, 'I can't lose it! I can't, I can't, I can't!'

'Calm down, calm down!' someone tells her.

Blue-white, blue-white. Hot, white sunlight. Burning soles. Yellow and red against a terracotta surface. Where's the shade? Look for shade. Marigolds and tinsel, the smell of incense.

In the wall of blackness, images appear. A woman on her knees, the sound of drums beating. She bends forward, her forehead touches the ground, she swings her body in a circular motion from the waist up, her long hair swings around. Rhythmically, slowly in a circle she moves and then faster and faster. Her hair fans out, swishing, around. She moves faster and faster, the beat keeps time with her. Dust clings to her hair as it sweeps it off the ground and throws it in the air all around her. Swish, swish, round and round. She does the dhamal.

'Who is she?' she asks.

'Who knows? Some poor woman asking for mercy.'

'Is she drugged?' she asks.

'No.'

'How do you know?' she asks.

'She isn't, not everything here has to be about drugs. She is praying, praying for salvation. She has come to this shrine to pay her respects to the sufi saint.'

'Not everything here has to be about praying. She seems intoxicated,' she retaliates.

'She is. On God.'

'Give me a break!' she sniggers.

'Take it.'

'Is she here on a pilgrimage?' she asks.

'Could be.'

'Is this for repentance?' she asks.

'Could be, or it could be for thanksgiving or for a heartfelt request, a desire for some fulfillment.'

'What kind of a woman would do this?' she asks.

'Any kind, just a woman, a mother, a

warrior, a lover, a sister, a wife, a whore.'

'Just a woman then. Anyone?' she asks.

'Yes anyone, princesses, noblewomen, prime ministers, fighters, whores, all of them have come to this shrine.'

'Do men do this?' she asks.

'I think so, but the image is always of women.'

'Why?' she asks.

'Don't know, maybe they have more to ask of God.'

'Do they?' she asks.

'Or maybe they're closer to God. Does that make you feel better?'

'Yes. Does it work?' she asks.

'What?'

'This public humiliation?' she asks.

'It's purgative, very cathartic.'

'Humiliating!' she says.

'Why do you consider it a humiliation? It's an expression.'

'Of what?' she asks.

'Agony and ecstasy.'

'Does it work?' she asks.

'Try it.'

'So which one am I?' she asks.

'Ah now, greater men than I have lost

our heads for answering that question, Madam!'

'Who am I?' No one answers. She raises her voice and screams till her throat burns.

'Who am I?'

There is no sound. Not even her own.

Who?

15

She's standing in a grocery store. She is crying, 'I can't lose it!'

Jack's face telling her, she can't lose it. 'This opportunity won't come again, you can't lose it.'

Blades are whirring. 'I cannot lose it! I cannot lose it!' she is sobbing.

There is an angry face talking. He is shouting. He is shouting at her.

Losing. Losing. Losing.

Portrait to the left, flag to the right.

At the stroke of dawn, one week ago, destiny beckoned, the blessed homeland called its patriotic sons, to once again serve its needs. At that hour, I had reported to you that the homeland was safe, and I made a promise to you, my dear countrymen, fathers, mothers, sisters, brothers, my children. I had promised you that we would always remain loyal servants and that we would safeguard this sacred soil to the last breath.

The last breath.

Breathe.

Breathe in, breathe out. Breathe in. Breathe out. Breathe.

Move. Lift yourself. Rise and rise and rise.

She floats. She falls.

There is a helicopter landing. She watches it come down. He is saying, 'I can't lose you.'

She watches the blades turn, they stir up the leaves on the ground, they cause a whirlwind, turning, churning, swirling, and whirling. She's turning and turning. 'I cannot lose you.'

16

There is a room with thick white carpeting and tall buildings in its windows. The walls are bare. There is Jack. There is a crowd of uniforms and suits.

You cannot lose, together we will make the country strong again.

Memory. What is happening?

'Who cannot lose?' she asks.

'I cannot lose you,' she hears his voice. 'I must not lose you,' she hears him say. 'Don't lose,' she hears him command her. 'Don't let them get there. Don't let them take that. Think. Remember.'

She remembered an article from the

City page in the newspaper, that she had read just the other day, she would use it as her cheat sheet to recall the way out. Remember it, remember it. Think hard about the article. Why did she remember it? What was her connection to it? Had she read the paper or a galley? Had she edited it? Yes, she had worked on it. He had mentioned that.

So you think you can rewrite anything?

'If it needs to be rewritten, yes.'

Flash of light. Fire.

Flood of red, growling, snarling, concussions.

Why had he hit her?

What was going on?

Did I edit it? I was looking over it only in yesterday's galleys. 'The route of the procession will be Nishtar Park, Sir Shah Nawaz Bhutto Road, Father Jaminis Road, Mehfil-e-Shah-e-Khurasan, Mohammad Ali Jinnah Road, Boulton Market Road, Bombay Bazaar, Kharadar and Nawab Mohabat Khanji Road.' It had caught her eye, the poetry of it had caught her attention, the poetry of the names, the history of it, beginning with humans and then losing itself in numbers and planning, Federal B, Defense, Buffer Zone, Phase I and II and VIII. The ebb and flow of movement, she had said to herself, she had wondered if the reporter writing it had felt as she had, reading it. There was a reason it had caught her eye.

From eclectic to order. Cleck, cleck tick, tick, cleck.

Now, she would use it, that article, and navigate herself, use it as her guidebook, negotiate her way, make it the route out of here, move through its map. What is that sound? She could hear weeping. Who is it? Is it herself, is she crying?

Or is it memory?

She listens, carefully, nothing. And then there is sound.

There is that sound, what is it, like metal scrapping? Metal, shinking? What is it? She hears metal.

Tin clinking.

Shink-shinking. Chink-chinking.

Knives.

She sees blood.

She smells it.

She stops it.

Stop that thought. Cannot. Remember, remember, go somewhere else. Knives, knives, shinking, clinking, chinking, catching the sunlight, slashing lines of blood on flagellated backs. This is a procession. There is a procession, she watches it, there are flags and there is mourning and yet it's a celebration. She is passing out. The sight of blood makes her turn. There are words.

Justice! Justice! Justice!

Pain.

She feels pain.

The questions begin.

Why?

'Why, what?'

Treason!

'How?'

Instigating rebellion.

She feels pain.

She asks for water.

Water.

Cold water hits her. Crashes against her, drenches her. Someone laughs.

Water. The shock of it, tells her that

her skin has split open, there are wounds, it sends her out of her skin, then just as quickly she crashes back in, sucked far in, till she is a speck. A dot. A yellow dot barely visible to herself.

There is the Attock Fort on the banks of the Kabul, can you see the bridge over the Kabul river? Water.

And that's the Lahore Fort on the banks of the Ravi. Water.

This is Sukkur jail. On the Banks of the Indus. Water.

And this was the Rawalpindi Jail.

And this is Kot Lakpath.

And this is Central Jail.

And this is the Lahore High Court. And that is the Sindh High Court. And this is the new Supreme Court building.

She'll never get across the Chenab tonight. The matka, the clay pot she uses to cross over every night has been replaced, the clay vessel that she picks up, in the dark of night, is unbaked. 'Don't you know, Soni, tonight you will drown trying to reach Mahiwal. You will drown in the river, Mahiwal will reach you, he will drown with you.'

Witness water. Sun rises, a flutter, light on water, a bird takes wing, then another, then all the others. Flutters, wings, rippling water. Light. Like that, like that, so bright. Khuda Hafiz, Khuda Hafiz.

17

A voice drowns out her delirium.

For ten years you have had no problem following our lead, and now what happened?

'What?' she asks.

What happened? Who is advising you? Old hag! Answer me!

Rebellion. Her stomach is turning, she's beginning to fall, there's so much blood, there's so much bleeding. She is rebelling against the shouting. A hand hits her, knocks her out again. There is sticky, warm red in her vision.

At the cash register.

At the procession.

In the room at the other end of the corridor.

So much blood so much bleeding.

There are crowds, there are banners, people pressing against her. People gathering, crowds, so many people. She must remain calm, I must remain calm, remain poised. Someone shouts her name. People are shouting out to her. Why are they calling me? They are shouting out her name. She knows this, she feels it, but what is her name? What is her name? She asks them, 'What is my name? Who am I?' They are calling to her in the crowd. They are laughing. She is losing herself in it. The procession. She must join in its ebb and flow, I must be carried with it. Like water, like that. Seven seas. 'When the Aryans came to this region from Persia they saw the mighty vast river and thought it was an ocean with six seas.'

Indus. Water.

Ravi. Water.

Sutlej. Water.

Chenab. Water.

Jehlum. Water.

Beas. Water.

Kabul. Water.

She is standing holding her mother's hand, they stand on a river's bank.

'All this water, Mother, where does it come from?'

'From there,' her mother points to the mountains.

'Where the snow is?'

'Yes.'

'Is that the beginning.'

'You can think of it that way.'

'Are there people there?'

'Yes.'

'Are they like us?'

'Yes.'

'Are we the ending?'

No one answers. She is alone again.

Darkness. No one answers.

'I must find my way, I must find my way to you,' she says.

'Find your way to me.'

'Your way, is my way?' she asks.

'*Rahe tu, rahe man.* Our paths are the same, what is my path is your path.' What was that line he had recited to her, what was that verse? How did it go? What was that song he would sing to her?

I must find your path.

'It's so cold here,' she says.

She is so cold here. Think light, think light. Flashes. White light that hurts. She stops the thought. First light, first light, dawn. No, think sun. Think sunlight. She had dreaded that first light the night she had been with him, she had loved first light when she had been with him, lying next to him just as the birds awakened to the light, watching the light grow over them, loving that moment, and dreading that it signalled his departure from her. When was that? Was it yesterday? Was it ever? Or was it only desire? Was that a dream, or did she live it? Did it matter? It was with her. It was there. Did she live those nights?

'Till tonight, my love, till night.'

'Is that all we have?' he asks.

'There is no other way.'

'There is but you won't take it,' he says.

'There is no other way.'

'Stay with me,' he pleads.

'Impossible,' she replies.

18

She is dragged, again. Through the corridor, out of the lying down room to the heated-lighted room. They undo the blindfold. The room is dark. The lights are off. She kneels, huddled, crumpled over, quietly. Waiting, for them to begin. Waiting for the lights to come on. She hears them leave the room, the door closes. Cleck, cleck, tick, tick. She hears this. Something is moving. Something moves, swiftly, on the floor near her. Something slithers over her foot. She kicks out, instinctively, naturally. She sits shaking. She knows. She knows. She knows. They know. She feels it crawling up her leg. She grits her teeth. Suddenly the lights go on. Her eyes lose the blackness and see nothing. She begins to focus, she is focusing only on her leg. She is right. There is a lizard, a gecko on her calf. She can only focus on it. Then as she beats her leg against the floor, she looks up and away from herself. The room is filled with lizards. All watching her. They have filled the room with lizards. How did they know? How did they know?

She is screaming and screaming. She falls back. She comes to. They are in her hair, they are on her legs. One slithers on her face, they are stuck to her. She's screaming and screaming. It's going to take forever, and ever and ever and ever and ever, she will never pass out. She will be conscious through this. She screams and screams and screams, she must pass out, she must reach hysteria, she must, she must, she must. She must go insane to keep her sanity, she must, she must, she must! Something snaps, the cord is disconnected, lights out.

Take her out! That's enough for now. Let's see what that does, shall we? Take her back.

Take me back.

Take me back.

Take me back.

I have seen in Bamiyan, Buddhas by moonlight. Giants in the mountain side.

Sharper than the edge of the sword and thinner than a hair. The House of Lies.

Those of my right hand, those of my left hand.

I have seen a mountain wounded, become a casualty of war.

Once peaceful, now defaced.

What wounds are these that must be healed?

Where lies the balm to heal?

I have seen moonlight gently kiss those delicate ripples of a limestone cloak.

Rock, folding into folds, like waves in a near still lake.

The center of the lake, the heart. A still pool shimmering beneath a cold silvery glow.

Hands in mudras,
Gestures of peace, peace, peace.
Reassure and provide,
Beneficient and Merciful,
Rehman and Rahim,
Echo of what has come,

Herald of what is to come.
The same spirit.
Who can erase this?
It's indelible.
It cannot be killed.
It cannot be burned.
It cannot be dynamited.
It cannot be eradicated.
It remains, it will remain.
Moonlight in Bamiyan. Light.
I felt light when I was with you.
Fresh clean sunlight.
Cold sunlight on a leap year morning.
Fresh clean sunlight,
Shadows validate light.
Winter light.
Light at a slant, at odds with me.
A bridge, I'm on it.
Sharper than the edge of sword and thinner than a hair.
Lightly, I touch its iron railings.
Iron railings, meant to prevent me from falling.
The bridge, the light, the rails and I.
Its iron rails' shadows slant on the sidewalk before me,   behind me.
Rails against me. Railings against me.

Where, I wonder, will these rise to meet me?

Rise to embrace me, surround me, cage me.

Sunlight casts shadows against me.

Light.

I felt light. Think light now, think heat. She screams and screams and screams, she must pass out, she must reach hysteria, she must, she must, she must. She must go insane to keep her sanity. 'I must! I must! I must!' She is shrieking. It is so loud. She is surprised at the sound of her voice, it's torn and hoarse, it's deep it's from somewhere else, somewhere inside, a place, places, she didn't even know. There are caverns we haven't discovered yet. Deep within us, did you know that, did you know?

19

She hears the shrieks of girls, there's laughter, there are giggles, the pain recedes.

It's getting better, it's going to be fine now, she tells herself. Think light. It's a December morning, the sun is shining, she is seated on the grass on the front lawn, at college. There they all are, her classmates. The one girl who just got married is there too, she's come back to college after her honeymoon, she's telling them she's going to finish her BA. Someone asks her what it was like. You know, the first time, the first night. Someone asks, 'Is there a bone in it?' More shrieks, more laughter. Lots of 'Ughs!'

and, 'Oh I'm going to be sick!'

'Is there a bone in it?'

'Ugh!'

'Did it hurt?'

Giggles. Shrieks of laughter.

'Oh sick, oh gross!'

'I'm never getting married!'

'Me neither!'

'As if you have a choice.'

'Take a valium beforehand.'

'Take several,' another chimes in.

'I'm going to get local anesthesia!' someone else chimes in.

And then everyone calms down, to learn whether there is or isn't one in it. 'Did it hurt?' More giggles, nervous laughter. Then, they move on and someone asks what would be the one thing that we could absolutely not do without if we were stranded on a desert island. Someone says, a tweezer, and they all nod in agreement, a girl, well groomed girls, such as they, simply cannot do without a tweezer, they all agree. And what is the one thing that they are all scared of? Well, everyone agrees, about the first time.

'Ugh! And what else? Lizards! Oh

God. Yes. Lizards! I know they'll be the death of me! I know I'm going to just die if one falls on my head. You know what happened to me once?'

'Oh no please don't tell us, I'm going to be sick!'

Don't think, don't think, don't think! Falling, falling, falling.

The sun is shining, the air is cool. She's got that ample green shawl from Anarkali draped around her.

'Lovely green. Is it a pashmina?'

'Of course not!'

'Looks like it is. It's so huge.'

'Guess how much?'

'No! Really? Unbelievable!'

'I know, isn't that great!'

'Don't tell anyone it's not a pashmina.'

'But it isn't.'

'Don't be so stupid, just lie.'

'Why?'

Hold the thought, hold it. The sunlight, the bright green on green, orange keenos, pockets full of dried fruit, the high pitched peal of laughter. It's gone. The green, the orange, hold on to it. Those morning assemblies and her arriving late for them, clipity clopping in smartly, on stilettos, painchas are tight this year, hemlines are long. Verrry long. She loves the part when everyone sings a hymn...then the Head Girl reads, 'The King of Mankind, the God of Mankind...' She can't keep the thought. It's cold here. It's damp under her, it's her, she's wet herself. Is it urine or is it blood? She can smell both. She feels shame.

She can barely see.

'Will my face ever be the same again?' she asks the assembly. The Head Girl says, 'The God of Mankind, the King of Mankind.'

What was her face? Was she the face she had recalled, the one in the lights?

Was that her?

Will my body ever be unbroken?

Will I live through tonight?

Will I be intact?

Will they let me go?

Will I?

Will I?

I will.

I will.

'Keep saying that. I will.'

'Urine heals,' he says, softly, kindly, gently.

She hears his voice, 'Urine heals.' There he is binding a white gauze bandage soaked in his urine on his swollen aching knee. She holds it down for him to keep it in place, suppressing her revulsion. And in the morning, his knee is fine. At first light, his knee is fine.

At first light, my spine will be fine.

At first light, my ribs will be fine.

At first light.

Does anyone know where I am?

How long has it been?

Has it been just a few hours, or longer?

She has no tolerance for pain. Even a moment of it seems to last forever. Then why does she always keep getting in its way?

Pain.

December morning, the girls are laughing at her, they're teasing.

'No, I don't!'

'Yes, you do, don't lie!' Peals of laughter. 'You think you'll get away. You think you're going to avoid it.'

The thought of pregnancies and labor frightened her. Well that didn't hold did it?

She had Iman and Aman in her own good time.

'Didn't I?' she asks everyone. They are all laughing.

Yes, of course she did. Just as she had planned she would. And that wasn't simple. No that was not simple. The physical part had been easy, she had seen other women, friends, relatives scream out in pain and plead for an epidural. She knew she would too, when the time came, and that's how it worked, she had started to holler for the epidural just when her water broke! Like water. Where is the water? She cannot see water. There is blood.

Where is the water? There should be water.

The flag flies. The national anthem plays. A scowling general appears with his chest thrust forward. The impossibilities of too many medals. A portrait in the background.

It's familiar, so familiar.

He speaks.

He speaks in English.

His accent is clear.

His tone precise and clipped.

He begins. He seems to hiss and clip his way through his words.

At the stroke of dawn, one week ago, Destiny beckoned, the blessed homeland called its patriotic sons, to once again serve its needs. At that hour, I had reported to you that the homeland was safe, and I made a promise to you, my dear countrymen, fathers, mothers, sisters, brothers, my children. I had promised you that we would always remain loyal servants and that we would safeguard this sacred soil to the last breath. And we have kept that promise. We have removed from power the irresponsible and flagrantly arrogant government that has brought our country to the brink of economic and social collapse. It has been a week since we have removed this cancer from our system. It is now time to restore order and decency. It is time to restore the constitution and a civilian government. I assure you that elections will take place as soon as we have assured that decent, honest and patriotic men and women offer themselves for service. In the meantime, we have searched the world, to find a patriot to head the country's interim government. Caste, creed, gender and ethnicity are not our concern. We are proud to tell you that we have convinced a decent, honest, intellectual human being with a vision, to lead you, someone that all of you admire and can be proud of to take up the position.

She seems to remember this. Was she watching this, listening to it? Was she reading about it, just before this happened? Before this dark room.

How long has it been? A day perhaps, a few days? She cannot tell, there is no light in this room and there is no window. She hasn't seen any windows. Only the darkness in this room and the bright lights in the other place. The other place. Between here and there, she knows there is space. There is a long corridor too, but she hasn't seen it. She has walked it and been dragged through it. And she doesn't know how she returned here.

'I hurt,' she tells the air around her. 'It hurts everywhere.'

There is no consolation.

Silence.

'I cannot hear, I think they've smashed my ear or my ear-drum,' she says out loud.

Her eyes are too swollen and she can barely open the lids.

'I need my glasses,' she says.

She never got the chance to get her

glasses on in time. It was probably for the best, they would have been smashed. They could have been smashed on her face.

'My glasses.'

She can see her glasses, they are sitting on her nightstand, on top of the novel that she had just put down. What was she reading? Remember it. She cannot. She cannot remember. The lamp is still on. What a lovely sight that is. Remember that sight. The soft, sweet glow of her bedside lamp shines off the pewter rim of her glasses. Her glasses are waiting for her. They will be there when she goes home.

'Home. It's going to be alright. I'll go back there.'

Silence.

20

It happened so quickly. She must have been dreaming. Someone came crashing through the door, she was pulled out of bed, then there were more people, more men. Someone held a pistol to her jaw, she remembered that clearly. She remembered, that she was concerned about the bruise it would leave.

'I'm afraid of guns. A gun can go off, even if you don't really want it to. Even if you don't want it to.'

It had.

What happened then?

She had looked up at a face. She had

seen that face before. Those eyes, ice. Iced-eyes. That face, it came to her now she had met it across the room on the forty-first floor with the view of Manhattan, all around them, as a backdrop, at every angle. And people angling for her mind. That person there, wearing that face, for just a moment, just as she had turned and caught his eye, caught him unaware. A blank face, a hard face, a deeply scarred look in a smooth scarless face. He had covered this face with the other face, the drawing room, charming, face. But the eyes remained, ice. Ice eyes. At that meeting when they came to make her an offer, plead their case and Jack stood in the background near a window, surveying the scene. History in the making. A scene for a history book. Perhaps Jack would write it.

There cannot be a better person.

'I am honored but I must,' she murmured, but was interrupted.

You are highly respected. Your character, your career, your record is irreproachable.

'Please,' she protested feebly.

You are known for your honesty, your integrity.

'That is why I must,' she tried again.

You have devoted your life singularly to the pursuit of truth.

'Please, you are making this very difficult.'

We intend to do that. Madam, your country needs you.

'My country has not asked, my country does not know me.'

You are wrong. You are known. And by the day after tomorrow everyone will know you. And besides we are its representatives! We are asking you.

She turns to look at Jack. But instead she catches the scarless-scarred face looking at her. Yes, you, yes him, the man in the room on the other end of the corridor, that face is there too, amongst those pleading the case, in their backdrop, his is there. Can it be called a meeting, between the two of them? No, it's a sighting. She has sighted him. And she is sighted by him, marked. She recognizes this. She feels the chill crawl through her. That face is familiar. It's a prototype. She has seen it flanking those that she has always hated. It weaves its way through the crowd in the room, sometimes here, sometimes there, sometimes hidden from view behind another head, sometimes to the side, ducking in and out, playing hide and seek with her anxiety. And later, she sees it flanking her in photographs. That sinister presence remains in the room. She learns that he is part of the IS. The 'Intelligence Service,' somebody whispers, then jokingly says that it's neither. Iced-eyes.

'You know, the intelligence service!'

'Which is neither.'

'Don't be so mean.' Giggling. Though it's a tired joke, but everyone titters anyway.

'You're calling me mean? Try them on for service some time.'

She can't share the mirth. She is frightened. He enters people's homes in the middle of the night, in the dead of night, and hurts them.

'He makes people disappear!' she hisses under her breath insistently.

'It's nothing personal,' the hostess says. 'He simply does his job. He's loads of fun otherwise.'

'He's here to look after us.'

And at some other time, he is there

beside her, in front of her. Barking orders at her in a low but firm voice.

Madam you will have to wear this jacket.

'It's ugly, its bulky, it makes me look fat,' she pouts.

Madam, it's bulletproof, it's for your protection. He has no humor.

'There must be some other way!' she insists.

Madam, I am simply doing my duty. Those are the rules.

Rules!

You do your job well.

When you came crashing in through the door. Everything happened so quickly.

Behave yourself!

And for a split second she was grateful, because you had shouted, 'Behave yourself!' at someone with you. Then she realized, it was at her.

For the sake of Aman and Iman.

Then she heard a shot.

Then she was knocked out.

Then the twins were screaming somewhere in the house.

Then she was shouting out their names.

'Aman! Iman!'

Then her mother was in the doorway and both of them were with her.

She remembers screaming, 'Don't touch them!'

The girls were screaming, 'Don't touch her!'

Her mother was screaming, 'Don't touch her!'

She was screaming, 'Don't touch my mother, don't touch my children!'

And then there was this.

What was this?

Where are they? She feels hysteria beginning. Did they take them too?

'I think I'm going to throw up! Oh God, I'm sick again! The stench of me, I can't stand my own smell. Where are they?'

Silence.

'Why don't you answer me? Are they somewhere like this?'

Silence.

'What have they been through?'

Silence.

'Surely not my mother, not my little

girls? Have I done this to them too? Why didn't I think of the consequences? It was not worth this.'

Silence.

'It was not worth it.'

Hysteria is beginning to rise again inside her. I cannot do that. I am so scared. Where are they? She had kept asking for them.

'Tell me! Where are my children? Where is my mother?'

She couldn't respond to any of their questions. All that was left was just this. 'Where are my children, where is my mother?' Just these two questions and for those they did this? What has happened? Can anything be worth this? Can there be any action deserving of this? Can writing really do this? Can a few sentences strung together in newsprint really do this? She must be dreaming. She must be dreaming one of those depressing movies that she never could sit through, avoided at all costs. Yet another film about the missing, the tortured. They seem to know so much, they know about her children. They know the details somehow. They know how they were born to her. Look what they've done to me. I cannot see it, but I can feel it. What will they say, what will they do now? They can't take me to a hospital, what will they say, she fell in the bathroom? It's too far gone for that. An attempted suicide?

You should have known better.

'Where are they?'

Didn't you learn anything, didn't you learn anything?

'Where?'

What do you mean where? You know very well what we mean. You're the bloody historian, the great big humanitarian!

21

This is not new. This is mine, familiar to me. This mist here, this valley. The pine trees, the smell of them. The scent of mist, the fragrance of earth. I have been here, the snow in the distance, those peaks in the distance that I am moving towards now, this is not new. This piece of earth, that everyone has opinions on, this is not new. It is mine. I am of it. They cannot take it from me. I will die here. I will die for it, on it. I will be in it. A part of it forever.

Where? Hypocrite! Focus, bitch! What are you talking about?

She passes out. Cadets. She is talking.

She hears herself droning on and on.

'If a principle is violated once and is allowed to be violated, it will continue to happen again and again. It is inevitable. Principles cannot be set aside. There are no caveats, ifs, buts, or maybes, no amendments, no abrogations, no extenuating circumstances, no invoking of any emergency powers.' And talking and talking. 'Those who uphold them are heroes and usually end up dead, unfortunately, and those who don't are hypocrites. Hypocrisy breeds. And it does so violently. We also tend to view and judge things depending on where we are located, individually, socially, and who our alliances are with. We never base our opinions, judgements or actions on the basis of principles, but rather on the basis of our alliances and our personal interests.'

She comes to.

'Where are they?' she repeats.

Traitor! Filthy traitor!

'What have you done?'

Helicopter blades, earplugs, a crowd waiting beneath. She is descending. There are cameras. She cannot recall. That night, when they came to get her, tonight, last night, before then. What was going on when they came? Was she watching television when they came to get her? She was reading. Was it in the book that she was reading?

A black and white photograph of her, flanked by men with strong jaws and dark reflecting glasses.

She hears sobbing. Her own sobbing.

'I've got to write to you, I've got to write to you. They are calling me names. How will I get in touch with you?' she had asked him, it was so many years ago.

He had said, 'You know where my home is.'

'Yes,' she had replied. 'But I will not be able to reach you there.' He had looked at her blankly unable to understand what she had meant. To him, he was easy to reach. He was not remote, or isolated. He was. He was where he was.

'You will find me, you will find a way.'

She could hear the sound of her own sobbing, in the darkness.

'I have no way, only words. And my words, will they reach you?'

Silence.

In what language?

All I really used to know is how to write, I wrote and moved on. There is no way to go back, I didn't write for that reason, I didn't write to reach you, I wrote to finish. I wrote to meet deadlines.

They said, they kept saying it was something that she had written. She had rewritten something.

'I've written something.' There is only silence. 'Dearest, I am writing to you. Each word will replace tonight. Carefully, I'll begin imprinting each word onto the memory of tonight. I must erase it, this memory of tonight, I must replace it. Must replace these broken parts, will you give me yours? Will you? Can I have your parts, while mine mend, can we share them? Did you read what I wrote? Did it reach you?'

'What is mine is yours,' she hears his voice.

Which part are you from?

'What?'

Someone laughs.

We didn't really look into that before?

'What?'

Where are you really from?

From the beginning and the end.

Portions.

Parts.

Parting.

Partitions.

Party.

Parties.

What is going on? Remember! Remember how to remember.

I must place myself far from all this, somewhere safe where they cannot reach me. Some place where I can go, of which they do not know. They know so much.

I must go somewhere safe, a place they do not know of. Breathe, breathe deeply, go with my breath, further and further away where I will be safe.

She breathes through the nose, it hurts, it hurts so much, it's burning and it's cutting all at once, she thinks it's broken, but she consoles herself that it doesn't matter, the nasal passage is functioning.

Take in the air.

Breathe clean air.

Take it in.

Take out the poison, through the mouth.

Empty out your lungs.

Oh God it hurts! My ribs!

She thinks her chest is broken. What are all these parts called, she wonders, what are their names? Why doesn't she know the names of all her parts? Why didn't she wonder about these things before, why was this not important, her parts, why didn't she learn about this first. Why was her mind crammed full of other irrelevant details of irrelevant things, names of streets, the existence of God, Article V (a) of Schedule 3. Why did she know these when she didn't even know her own parts. Her whole body, what was it? She was going with her breath, riding it, letting it take her up, floating with it. She could see something, what was it that was beginning to emerge in her vision? Look. There it is.

There is a place, where there is a window, it overlooks a meadow full of flowers, they are yellow, big yellow wild flowers, like bottle-brushes on long stalks, and petals, purple and blue ones shaped like stars. Blue star flowers on a green grass sky. There is a place with a window and she can see outside it. She is inside, still inside, a place, looking out. She must get out. But for now this place with a window is okay. It's early summer or late in the spring and beyond the meadow is the river and beyond that the mountains with the snow and she could see the single minaret with the blue dome against the snow. She feels joy at this sight. It cools her, she presses its blueness, the yellowness, the whiteness, the coldness of the snow against her wounds and the pain begins to subside. It will subside. She tells herself. She hears him shout out to her with excitement, 'Snow up to here!' His hand is next to his waist. She sees a glimpse of him, he is dancing in the snow, arms outstretched, he moves his shoulders and hips. He motions to her to join him.

She whispers, 'I am trying. Like water. I am mostly water, too, I'll evaporate, into moisture and become the snow on your mountains. I'll come out to you, as snow.'

Her mother points to the mountains in the far distance. 'See it snowed over there.'

'Snow like on television that children make snowmen out of?'

'Yes. Like that.'

'Can we go there?'

'It's too far away.'

'Is that place on the moon?'

'No.'

'Is it here?'

'Some of it, yes.'

'Where is it?'

'Those are the Hindu Kush mountains and beyond that the Pamirs.'

'How come we can see them if they aren't here?'

'We can see them, but they are beyond our borders.'

'What are borders?'

'Borders make countries.'

'I want to be snow. Become snow.'

She must move quickly, she must get there, she must access it. She must remain intact. The pain and ugliness of everything could now seep in, take over, and settle in, if she doesn't move quickly. This face, her face, she cannot see it, is smashed, she can feel it and this body is wrecked, she does not remember after the first hour, what it was that they were hitting her with, was it their fists? She cannot remember. I don't want to remember. They are against sinning. But they are for punishment. They punish sinners, with sins. They think they have reached me, but they have not. I will not let them get any further. They do not know this, they do not know. I know, because I heard their voices as I was lying on the floor as they gathered around to figure out what to do next.

She isn't moving!

Is she breathing?

She's bleeding!

Laughter.

That's a sign.

Throw her back for a while.

But, what if…

What if? What if, what? Do as I say!

They sounded afraid, they thought they had gone too far, they were debating what to do next. She thinks they cannot really say she did this to herself. So they will have to keep her here till she begins to heal. But who knows what they are capable of. They can say anything, no one seems to question anything. Except them, except him. He has lots of questions for me.

What did you think you were doing?

'What?'

Do you see what you've done!

'What?'

See what you made us do?

'What have you done?'

The Supreme Court and other courts will continue to function as long as they don't contradict us.

He grinds his words, through his teeth.

'You can't...'

I said, don't contradict us...

Crack goes her cheek-bone. Her mouth spits teeth, lips bleed, and tongue grows and twists. Twists, turns, blisters, burns. And twists and twists.

You should not have resisted us, we are not against you. You know that. We brought you.

'You brought me here?'

Not just here, everywhere! You are nothing without us.

'What?'

And you thought you could turn against us? Weaken us? Did you think we would allow it? We made you,and we will end you. Madam you are a traitor. You thought you could go for a stroll across the border and embrace the enemy? What did you think you were doing? Taking a stroll in Oxford or Cambridge? Harvard, or Columbia? Hyde Park or Central Park?

'It's not safe at night in Central Park,' she says.

We have the national security to protect. Borders to protect. Your philosophical ideas do not protect borders. Borders are protected by us.

'Why protect the border? Why have borders?'

Traitor! Just listen to her!

As though he has obtained a confession.

Look at me. Open those eyes. That's right, look at me. This is the face of a faithful, patriot. I froze on glaciers with my friends. I gave the order to move forward and I charged into battle with them. And they followed without once questioning me. Without so much as flinching. Total trust, total belief, total obedience. A cause, one true cause. Defense of the homeland. We will protect it to our last drop of blood, we believe this. And while we are dying up there in the mountains, in the snow, in the ice, you are here in the plains, indulging in the luxury of ideas, philosophies of what should be and what shouldn't be. I know just one thing, I was asked to defend this country and follow orders and I did that. And I will always do that. You think that you can get away with this, rewrite the constitution, cut away our power, reduce the defense of this country, open its borders?

'You can't make honey without travelling.'

What?

Laughter.

'And snow. You can't get to the snow.'

What is she blathering about?

'Bees don't understand borders.'

What?

'Eyes don't understand borders.' Except, of course, iced-eyes.

She passes out.

22

She is sitting on a pile of rugs. The shop is a small one. The shopkeeper pours her milky tea into a glass from a blue tin kettle.

'Where are you from?' she asks.

'Mazar.'

'How much for this one?'

'Oh this one is for two thousand.'

'Is it a Hazara.'

'No it's a Turkoman.'

'In Bamiyan have you seen the Buddhas in the side of the mountains?'

'Yes.'

'How are they?'

'Wounded.'

'And this one?'

'A Balochi.'

'This one?'

'Tabrazi.'

'How much?'

'Fifty thousand.'

'So much!'

'Two hundred years old.'

'And what's that on the wall?'

'A suzana. From Ferghana.'

'Ah yes, the cherries.'

'Those are pomegranates.'

'Like those from Kandahar?'

'Yes.'

'And that?'

'A phulkari.'

'And this?'

'An ajrak.'

'And this?'

'A pashmina from Kashmir or Nepal.'

'Kashmir, it's fine, you see, how fine?'

'From the Caucasus to Kashmir to Karachi, all in your little shop!'

'Yes and everything for sale! Begum Sahib make up your mind.'

'Do I have to?'

The colors fade, sadness creeps in with the pain. Grief. I must go. It is so dark in here, it's so cold. The space around me is wet. Is it me? My body weeps, I can smell my body weeping blood.

Answer me!

'What should I tell you?'

You will talk sooner or later.

'Where are Aman and Iman?'

Who?

'Where is my mother?'

What crisis were you trying to create?

'Where are my children?'

Why are you creating trouble like this?

'Please.'

Don't you love this country?

'Answer me!'

No you answer me, you bitch. I ask the questions. Do you understand? Who do you think you are?

'Who am I?'

Do you think you can rewrite whatever you please?

'What?'

You cannot change what we've worked so hard to establish. If you ask why, you are a traitor! You are a traitor if you question! You cannot question it! You cannot change it! If you try, we will wipe you out. But first we will establish you as a criminal. Everything you accuse us of, we will accuse you of, and hang you with it. Do you understand? Read that. Write that. Try re-writing that.

They said I wrote. I am confused. I must be important. The editor of an important daily newspaper, disappeared? I read that. Didn't I? Was that me? Am I the one? They say I've written something, I'm changing something. Surely, there must be an uproar about it outside these walls. They say I've written something and they will ban me. Did they say they would ban me, or did I read that? What did they say to me? They said they would rip me apart.

Was she paper, was she a document? They say they've done it before, they will do it again, easily. Outside, does anyone know what's happening? Do they even know yet? Would they understand? Would they care? How long has it been, is it just tonight, is everyone asleep, does the night seem long only to her, has she lost count of the hours, lost her orientation.

'I need my glasses.'

Write. She tells herself.

'This will be my last dispatch for the night, stop press, I have one last piece to submit. I need to tell you how. How much, how much I do. How much I wanted to.'

'How?' she hears him ask softly.

'I don't know how.'

23

'You should have children,' she hears him say.

'Children?'

'Don't you want children?' he asks.

'I can't.'

'Why not?'

'Not now, I have so much to do.'

'Don't say that,' he says.

'Okay, I won't say that, if it makes you happy.'

'We should have had children.'

'We?'

'Yes, we should.'

She cries out in despair, 'I should have stayed.'

'I think their main purpose was to scare me, just rough me up a bit so that I would stop writing the editorials. But then they opened the file on me. And they found that Aman and Iman were my daughters. They found out about our little girls.'

He asks, 'How did that happen? No one was supposed to know.'

'They knew! They knew. They were saying their names,' she says.

'Did you tell them they were mine,' he asks.

'No,' she says.

'You should have. They should know. I will come for them. I will kill them for what they have done to you.'

'But I told them you were dead.'

'Why?'

'I told them we were married. You know to protect the girls.'

'Good.'

'The girls will be safe that way,' she says.

'I am sad,' he replies softly. His voice is graveled, she can tell how grieved he is by the sound of his voice.

'I couldn't tell them the truth. The girls would suffer!' she protests.

'I am sad,' he repeats.

'I couldn't have just said the children were mine and there was no one else. I could have said that I had adopted them, but if they were going to kill me I didn't want Iman and Aman to be left thinking that I was not their mother. I asked for them and someone called me a bitch in heat. They laughed.'

Bitch in heat!

She's itching for a litter.

Well, well, well so she thinks she has children. Good work boys, you're doing a fine job!

Have a few for me too.

The only place to be was nowhere and unconscious, through this. She knew she must leave now, she must. Where should she go? Home? Where is that?

'Where are my children? Where is my mother?'

They are safe.

Why did he say, *So she thinks she has children?*

'I do. Don't I?'

They are all safe, they are all together.

And where should I go? Now? To them? No, it would shatter them.

The children should not see her this way. Neither should her mother. Her family, her friends would come for her. Jack would come for her, she was sure of it, they were looking for her, she knew it, she could feel it.

'But I must be safe until they find me. I must be there when they do reach me.'

There? Where?

'There, intact. I must be intact. All the parts of me, they will piece together. They will put me back together. Those parts of me, will find me. Where should I go until they come? To the house? Yes, to the house then, I must turn my gaze.'

House? What house is that?

The place with the window? She doesn't know. But she sees it. There is a mist, it's rising. It'll be early morning there, she doesn't know why but she thinks it will be early morning. Light hits the stones, beautifully at first light, everything is golden peach. Light on her skin, somewhere golden peach. The kind of light that makes flowers perfume, fruits fragrant, lovers passionate.

She is floating above the meadow, her gaze comes in towards the house. Wait, there's a deer in the meadow, he is looking towards the house, he is standing there alert, and then suddenly darts away into the mountains, he must have felt her presence. She moves on towards the house. Someone is up, it's early in the morning. They are together in that place of only good. Good. Only good. They're planning, as they lie in each others arms, they're going to come and get her. They will reach her, rescue her. They're coming. They know. They'll come soon.

24

Asma watches him across the dining table from her. Her fingers pick at and smoothen out the delicate embroidery, mauve and pink, on the tablecloth. She had had it made at the Army Wives' Industrial Home. He looks up at her, his eyes are taking her in, he smiles. She notices that he has smiled self-consciously. He doesn't do that. His mouth quivers at the ends, his voice is gentle, 'I like that color, it looks good on you. Yellow and red, I like that on you.' He lowers his eyes, lifts the teacup to his mouth.

'Humza?'

He doesn't look up at her. His hands are shaking. He forces himself to take a gulp and sets it down with a clatter.

'Humza.' He can hear the fear in her voice.

He looks at her, then at the cup, he focuses his stare at the cup and on his two hands resting on either side of it.

She sees his shoulders hunch over and she realizes he is crying silently. Asma rises in panic, turns to check where the children are, they are still outside playing, 'What's the matter Humza, what is it, what's happened? What's happening, what's the matter?'

Humza leans against her and his sobs are muffled against her belly. 'I can't, I couldn't do anything!'

'Humza what are you talking about? What has happened?' She tries to maintain her balance, one arm around her seated husband the other hand on the table to steady herself. They remain that way. He clutches her around the waist, he sobs, he uses her dupatta to wipe his face.

'Humza?'

He won't look up at her.

'Humza!'

He can hear the fear rising in her voice. He looks up. His face at this moment reminds her of their daughter right after a fight with the neighbors' kids. Asma feels love flooding her.

'Asma, the father had her killed!' Humza says.

'Humza what are you talking about? Who was killed?'

'Remember I told you about those feudal bastards who kidnapped and raped the girl. The father had the girl killed, so that he could protect the landlord, because we got involved! Right in front of our eyes!'

'What? How could that happen?' Asma was incredulous.

'It happened! The father agreed, because he could hardly say no to me, a major in the army. I wanted to bring the girl in with us for questioning and to get her statement recorded. She got into the jeep ahead of ours, with her father and two brothers. Half way down the road, we hadn't even left the village, they sped up, we lost them for less than a minute. When we reached them, their jeep had stopped, they said they had been ambushed. I should've seen it coming. The girl's throat was slit, it happened in a flash, yaar, and of course the murderers had disappeared. And of course the father and the brothers hadn't seen their faces. No one else was even slightly injured. The honorable thing had been done. And we couldn't do a damn thing. The girl's father had begged us to leave, said it was none of our business. We had left him with no other choice.'

'I can't believe this! I don't believe this,' Asma whispers.

'He had to do what he did, or right after we left the entire village would have been set on fire.'

'Humza, this is absurd, you're the military!'

'Yes.'

'I can't believe it.' She hurries on to say, 'But its not your fault.' She holds his head against her again, she's a good friend, a good wife.

Sunlight on water, blood drops.

25

'And Jack? What can Jack do now?'

The shouting begins again. They're laughing about Jack? 'Don't say that about Jack. Jack loves me. He's my friend. I'm his friend. I could learn to love him. Jack will find me, and Jack will come for me. He has rescued me before. This too will happen.' She passes out.

She hears Jack's voice, she is lying in the deck chair eyes shut against the beauty of the blue ridge in the distance. Is it the Blue Ridge? Or the hills of Ladakh or Gilgit, Garm or Swat? She cannot place it.

There is light shimmering on a blue-green surface, light on water. She is dozing off.

'I love you like that.' It's not Jack's voice.

'How?' she asks.

'Like light on water,' the voice whispers and fades away.

Then there is Jack.

Jack whispers, 'Will you stay tonight?' Jack asks an innocent question, nothing more. Eyes still shut, she imagines it to be him, his entreaty, she smiles, she turns her face slowly towards him, she open her eyes, but there is Jack's face, and she says yes to Jack. Words meant for someone else, she says to Jack.

'I'll stay.'

'Will you stay tonight?' he asks.

'Yes, I'll stay.'

'Oh goody, she'll stay!' Jack jokes.

'I could be pregnant, Jack.'

'Oh goody she's pregnant and she'll stay the night.'

Jack is angry.

She tells Jack that she could be pregnant. She tells Jack about him. And

Jack reaches out and takes her hand. He always has.

'You will take care of it,' he says.

'What do you mean?'

'You cannot do this!'

'I will.'

'Then you'll have to marry me,' he decides.

'Why?'

'How else are you going to do this?' he asks.

'There are scores of women in this country, who do.'

'You are not them,' he interrupts.

'No.'

'Please, let's do it,' he pleads.

'Do what?'

'Marry,' he replies.

'No.'

'It's right.'

'No. I act for love and never for necessity.'

Jack is hurt.

'Oh no Jack, I didn't mean...'

'It's alright,' he says.

'I love you, there is no need for anything more. Utility has always sickened me. I am surrounded by it. Obligations and utility. All that I must live up to.'

Jack fades away.

'Don't go Jack!' she calls. 'Don't go please. I need you here. I need you to understand.'

But it's black again. And she is cold again. Thinking about Jack.

She is at the grocery store. At the cash counter, someone behind her grabs her shoulder and shakes her. She turns to look at a terrified face. The man points to her feet. She looks down, she's standing in blood.

Jack, holds her. Wipes away her tears. 'There will be a next time,' he says.

'There is no next time. I had my chance.'

'You can try again,' he consoles her.

'I can never try again.'

'We can,' he says.

'No!'

The tone of her no, is not the way she wanted it to be. He receives the sounds of anger and revulsion.

Jack is hurt.

'You can say no to them. You can go

back to him,' his voice is edged with sarcasm.

She ignores the tone. 'Please Jack be realistic. Can you see the headlines for that?'

'Please, love, for once be human and not headlines.'

'This from you, Jack?'

She retreats. Recoils, retreats from Jack. Even Jack. Jack who cannot understand. She must go to a place where he can find her, intact. When her children, her mother, finally come for her she must be intact.

'I do have children.'

Laughter. Coarse, ugly, raucous laughter.

Why did they laugh?

When the children come for her, she must be intact. They must be able to recognize her. She must be as she was.

'As I was, as I am, as I left you.'

She does not want to remember these faces here. She does not want to remember their words, sentences without feeling, without emotion. She hears his voice.

'I understand you,' he whispers. 'I understand the sound of your voice, I know what you are saying by the look on your face.'

'You are free and you are without fear.'

'And you are here with me.'

'They cannot touch you. Stay with me.'

She weeps. She tries to say, 'I will', but someone is causing her pain, and snarling ugly words at her, calling her names. She lets herself slip away where they cannot find her.

There is the sound of poetry. The poet weeps. He is holding on to her. She is crying. She remembers, she has memory of it. He held her as she cried.

She focuses on the tears, she must hold on to them, they are the stream that will lead her home, safely back. The stream that opens into the pond, the pond with the luminous fish, where God spoke with her. The fish transform, become beautiful children. Two little girls. Her precious girls. Where she saw Aman and Iman splash about, swing from the rope and bomb the water with their four year old bodies. Paradise. She saw them in the pond, even before she had conceived them.

She saw them in the water.

Her memory. She only wants to remember those that are hers. Those that belong to her.

That which stays, is.

That which the mind can recall, was.

Plans, desires, dreams. The mind and memory. The only possession. No one can take that. You cannot part from it. You cannot be parted from it. You belong.

'No one belongs to anyone.'

'You belong to me,' he whispers.

'No.'

'Yes, you do!' he insists.

'How? Prove it.'

'You will see,' he says.

'When?'

'You will see, I will be all that there will be,' he repeats.

'When?'

'When there is nothing else.'

'Just you?'

'Just me.'

26

Memory. There are lullabies to remember and there are bedtime stories, a wedding song and the color of lime green with deep aubergine purple. And the yellow wild mountain flowers. Blue stars on green sky, flowers.

What is there to remember? What is there through which to remember? Scars, marks, seasons, colors, smells, sounds. From her window on Central Park West an autumnal park down below, greeted her as though a bride, with palms upturned, painted in mehndi colors. The season had turned but the colors it seemed, were waiting for her to return, before they began fading. She examines the mark on her forearm. A bruise, in the colors of an aubergine. She had wanted him to leave a mark. She must have memory of this, there must be something. He had drawn back to inspect the bruise on her skin, and then he kissed her harder biting her with his lips and teeth on her neck, then drew back to see the blue begin, then her shoulders, then her arms. She watches the bruises begin, wondering how love and hate can sometimes look the same. It fades. Memory fades. It's dark and she shivers. There is a stream, it's trickling out of her. Is it air, is it water? Like water.

She must go, to that place of waterfalls and fountains, of pure clean waters rushing down mountain gorges. She must ride those waves. Ride the wave, stay with the thrill, balance on it, just so, watch the churning and tumultuous white water, balance on its wave. She must go back to that place where she made her choices, where she made her decisions. She was going to keep her child. And she announced it in the middle of a coffee shop close to midnight.

'I'm telling you this, I will keep the child.' She blows the foam on the top of her de-caffé latté, and looks across at Jack's angry face.

An angry Jack face. She is angry too, at his face.

'Sorry. Calm down,' she says.

'No, I won't. How could you even think of it? Have you no sense! No sense of responsibility!'

'I thought you said don't try to be history. Live.'

'I said headlines, and don't distort our conversations!'

'You're angry with me. I'm keeping my child.' She repeats this, 'I'm keeping my child,' and then louder for everyone to hear. 'I'm keeping my child!'

A man reading a newspaper, emerges from behind it at the table next to theirs, 'I'm happy for you.' His sarcasm lifts their spirits and they laugh. They are grateful to him, he has momentarily united them.

'You haven't thought this through,' Jack says.

'There is nothing to think about.'

'Think, please, think,' he pleads.

'If I think it through the answer will be no,' she replies.

'This is not an adventure in some godforsaken mountain somewhere, with equally godforsaken bands of rebels. You can't return from this. This will not get done, like a story, filed and finished. Please think this one through!'

They fight, there are things said that should never be said.

'I don't want to be lectured by you,' she says.

'What do you expect from a professor,' he replies.

'You aren't a professor to me, for godssake,' she protests.

'Yes I am.'

'A friend,' she says gently.

'Your professor. Old.'

'Friend,' she insists.

'Yes, a friend. Meaningless.'

'Don't be that way! You know you are everything. My everything,' she says.

But he is hurt and he is angry. She listens, because everything Jack says is right. Everything Jack says about her, is exactly right. But she's going to keep to her decision.

Jack's message on the voicemail. Of course he is hurt. But it's too late. Jack should have acted sooner. Jack, too upright, too uptight. And she, just like Jack.

Just like Jack.

And he. He is not like Jack, not like her, not like them. He is not like Jack and she.

'How?' he asks.

His gentle soft kind eyes.

His face full of love for her.

His face turned towards her in open expectation.

His happiness to be in her presence.

His adoration for her.

His sheer joy of seeing her.

His calling her his princess.

His calling her his teacher.

His calling her his lover.

His calling her his partner.

His declaration, first there is God, then there is you.

Only you.

He blasphemes for her.

He sins for her.

He will burn for her.

He will fight for her, live, and die for her.

And Jack won't.

Jack will think things through. Jack will have seen other examples, everything has been done before, experienced, documented, analyzed, there are several references, he'll give them to her. He'll assess the consequences of it all, he'll walk around the issue. He'll provide options. And he'll call it all melodrama.

'For love,' she hears him say. Not Jack, no Jack will not say that. She hears that gentle voice, that sweet voice say to her. 'That is all there is, just love, remember that. Stay with me, stay here with me.'

And she won't. Because she is like Jack, she thinks things through.

Jack and she are thinkers.

Big thought thinkers.

Pontificators.

They are planners.

List makers.

Article publishers.

Public speakers.

Lecture givers.

Theory makers.

Paradigm breakers.

Award takers.

Art collectors.

Schedule keepers.

And added to this, she always leaves.

She watches the helicopter coming down to land. She has a schedule to keep. She has places to go. She has lists to make. She has a familiar, comfortable, predictable, respectable world to re-enter. She has a friend, a teacher, someone who understands, someone who will always leave the light on for her, and be there when she needs someone to be there. When she's out there.

But in here? No, Jack is not this. He cannot be. He doesn't fit. Jack does not fit. Not like him who fits, he fits so well, but in this space, only in this space. Not everywhere. Not then. And now, now, it's the only space left, it's all there is, there was nothing else. Too late, she never understood that this was the only space that mattered. Did he know that, did he know that all along?

Darkness. Not a sound. Just her breathing. Just the throbbing.

27

The space. Now the sum total of that space is this. Can it all amount to this?

On one end of a corridor is the interrogation room. On the other, solitary confinement, darkness and living with pain. In between, a corridor. I am dragged through it blindfolded from one to another. Was this why I am? Is this why I was? I am, I am, I am. Raised to serve, to be a martyr. To be jailed, to become an ideal. Looking back, down that corridor what will I recall? In that space what will there be? You coming towards me. As I unlocked the door to my room the door several doors down the corridor opened and you stepped out as though this were planned. You came down the length of the distance between us, swiftly. And as you walked down the corridor towards me I couldn't even smile and neither did you. As I entered my room my hand still on the door, you covered it with yours. And you entered.

But pain stops her. She recedes into darkness.

She resolves that she will write to him. I am writing to you and I will mail this letter. Once I get out of here. It will never reach you. Of course it won't. The thought of this breaks her heart. Her heart breaks inside her broken body, she visualizes it and the thought of it, her heart breaking, causes pain more unbearable than the broken flesh and bones.

'A heart's shape, within a shape of the heart.' She had said to him that it can't be love if it doesn't break your heart and it can't be poetry if it doesn't heal it. And he had looked at her with sadness and had shaken his head in sorrow.

'You don't understand,' he had said to her. 'It can't be love if it breaks your heart.

Love is joy, love is happiness, love, that's all there is.' That's what he had said to her. It came so easily to him. Poetry came to him.

'Do you know what that means?' she had asked him. And she had said, 'You are a human being, the very best kind.' And he had stopped her, flinching, saying that her words were meaningless to him. As she struggled with words, he had stopped her for her pointless pointing out of things, for her making grand statements, labeling him and his emotions.

'Why do you think that you can judge, why do you think you must say such things,' he had said. 'Why do you always feel the need to pass judgements, reach conclusions? Who are you talking to?' He had stopped her with a recitation from Hafiz, a verse, 'Wisdom, beloved, is the realm of those who speak sparingly and listen generously.' She had wanted to take back her words and convey to him what she had meant, no judgements, only gratitude, somehow to register that this meant more to her than anything else ever would. She tried to reach him.

'I too write poetry,' she had said.

'Recite something.'

She does.

'You are simply speaking your poem to me,' he said.

'What?'

'Words. Feel it to me. Let me hear the sound of your emotion.'

He is silent.

'Feel,' he says.

She begins again.

'Why do you cry?' he is baffled.

'Because, this is all there is. And this is not enough.'

Did she say that this would not sustain her? An absence of words would not sustain her. She wanted to be able to speak and say so much to him. The things she wanted to say, and yet she was so anxious because she did not have a language with which to get through to him.

'Forgive me my speech,' she had said, 'but I must do as I must do.'

'No! Speak with your eyes, your expressions, your hands, your tone, the movement, it will tell me,' he had said. 'I can tell by your eyes what you mean, and if you mean it. By the sound of your voice, I understand everything.' He had always said to her, 'Language of words, speaking words, can only go so far.'

The shouting begins.

You are lying, I can tell by the look on your face. I'll teach you a language you'll understand.

Oh God, the pain.

What did you mean to achieve by creating a crisis, who is paying you to do this?

She struggles. Push it out, push it out. She must not think of that. There was not time now to think of that. And into the darkness she spoke, 'I'm thinking only of you, not the room at the end of the corridor outside the steel door, outside this darkness. Yes, yes, that's what you had said to me, I understand that you are true, by the look on your face, I always knew. I knew that too about you. And it's true I too had understood what you had said about Hafiz.'

'What's wrong?' he asks.

'Nothing is wrong.'

'Then why the tears?' he asks.

'Perhaps because everything is right.'

'Everything is right. Don't think so much,' he laughs.

Would he remember? Would he remember that she did understand, the sound, his feelings, that poetry, she did understand, but she knew that he would never believe this if she were to tell him this to his face. If she could have said it to him, that is, but she couldn't have because her Russian didn't go that far and neither did her Farsi but with the combination of the two she had managed, she had groped her way through the pathway to him, accessed the road map and managed to navigate her route and convey her meaning. She remembered he had said that she shouldn't worry and that he understood what she was saying as she had stood in front of him, casting about for phrases, words, innovations, wringing her hands, straining every cell of creativity, playing charades and struggling with meanings. He said her name in the diminutive as he had taken to doing. He told her not to worry; and that he understood.

28

The first time she had seen him, she remembered, she had been irritated by him and actually a bit nervous and scared. The guns and his display of them frightened her, the long hair down to his shoulders and the beard. A soldier of God.

'A mujahid.'

'A murid,' he had corrected her.

And who was she? She, who was she? Someone important, visiting? There, to write his story? What were they, really? Both of them? She had asked herself. How was she seen and understood. How had he seen her and how had she seen him. Perceptions.

Deceptions. Misconceptions. She remembered his face, so dear, so soft, so kind and generous. The face that filled her with joy, how could she have possibly have ever thought of him any other way. But she had. She had thought in other ways.

There were history books read.

Music listened to.

Movies seen.

Photographs in newspapers.

News analysis.

Statements.

Editorials.

She was full of them.

There had been no other way to perceive.

How had he seen her, when he first saw her?

She remembers. The helicopter has landed. She is getting out. He sees people moving. He is walking towards her. He says something, she cannot hear him over the din of the helicopter blades. She motions to him to come closer. He doesn't. The noise stops abruptly.

He says he will be her guide, he stands at a distance. She comes closer, he stops her as though he is afraid that she will come too close. She stops, takes a step back. He stares at her. Then he says something. She cannot hear him. She asks him to repeat what he has just said. He looks at her and says he has a sister, her name is Fatima, she is his twin. 'I am sick, I don't want to make you sick. I have a fever.'

'I cannot hear you!'

'I have a sister, a twin, her name is Fatima.'

She looks at him. He stands at a distance from her. She takes a step towards him, she reaches out her hand and touches his forehead. Yes, she says, he has a fever. He must keep warm. She keeps her hand on his forehead as their eyes meet, in recognition. This is what he had chosen to say to her.

And that was it. He had done it, he had captured her. More than any other way of captivating her, it had been that simple. She had come home.

He takes her to the places she wants to visit. They walk, through mountain trails. They talk. He tells her about the story of the mountains, the people, their war. She learns that she does not like herself, her judging gaze that till now only sees a fierce soldier, strapped with carbines and shouldering a Kalashnikov. She knows that she cannot separate him from another part, another half an identical identity, a sister, a woman. A soft beautiful, green-eyed twin, she imagines, who has two beautiful little daughters.

Had he said daughters? What were their names? She could not recall. Two daughters? Had he said that? Why was her mind unable to focus? Again, memory faded in and out. When had the helicopter landed? Where had it landed? Why was she there? It was the beginning of autumn in the mountains and someone leaning over to her as she gazed out on to the crowd below and shouted, 'Wow! They are really going to give you a welcome, the whole nine yards!' And much later, much beyond the helicopter, there are caravans of jeeps and sirens and drums and women in colorful headscarves.

There is a press of people and someone shouts, 'Give way!' And she is fainting, falling, sinking. She opens her eyes, there are faces above her, peering down at her. Have they finally come to get her? No, she is there, still there in the mountains, she is fainting and falling and sinking. Her vision is blacking out again. She is in a grocery store and people are looking down at her. The faces look worried. She is bleeding. Jack said take care of it. And now, it was taken care of anyway. She holds the memory, the image, it emerges out of the dark, the room lights up and there is nothing else. Just his face.

His face looks down at her. The light, the joy the look on the face of the beloved, as she comes to. No one had looked that way on seeing her, other than her two daughters. Did he say his sister had two children or did he say she had two daughters?

The look. The sheer joy in that face.

Later he will ask her to stay.

'Don't go back, you are here. Stay with me.'

'You would never ask me to leave?' she asks.

'To leave? The thought is unbearable,' he says.

'I am glad.'

'That it is unbearable for me?' he asks.

'Yes.'

'To be without you?'

'Yes.'

To be without her. He had been overwhelmed by this and only focused on the fact that he would be without her. And she had replied as only those who are used to departing do, as only the selfish do, as only the greedy and the marauding can.

'Live now, think only of now. In this moment I am here.' That is what she had said.

And he had replied, 'I cannot, there will be a tomorrow.'

'There is nothing else but this, there is no future and no past.'

'I cannot,' he had insisted.

'It is all in the present.'

'I am thinking of tomorrow.'

'Be here with me now.'

'I am.'

'Be with me, at this moment.'

'I am here with you, now.'

'That is all there is.'

'But tomorrow I shall be here alone,' he had said sadly.

'Don't lose this moment, thinking about what has not yet occurred,' she said.

And he replied, 'I will miss you.'

'Do not miss me yet, I am here with you.'

'I will grieve.'

'Do not be sad while I am here with you.'

She felt it. This was love. That perfect moment. That rush. That's the secret, that's the way out of here, to be able to remain buoyed up in that current. In that moment. If only there was some way to maintain this moment with him, to not lose it. She recalls her hand on his forehead, the look in his eyes. That look, the recognition. That space between them. That's all that there is.

29

That place. A place of endless gestures, emotions expressed in touch, replacing words, making the tongue obsolete for words, essential for sense. What place was this? What space was this? Where was this, where thoughts were expressed with eyes, hands, eyelashes, lips, tongue, teeth, and breath? What place was this where these could not be compensated with words?

That place, where you are. Where I am filled with such intoxication, such exhilaration. That place where I have no burdens, no weight, where gravity ceases, and I am liberated. Where is that place for me?

That place in which she had arrived, without words, unable to speak, not a single notion, not a single clue. Not understanding words, not understood in words. This had locked her into a freedom, she would be understood regardless. There was more to understanding than words. And when she did use them they were without gender, without past, without future. She had functioned in the infinitive and if pushed, in the present.

To love.

To live.

To be.

With you.

Whatever the gender of the noun it found its true identity as it rolled off her tongue and attached itself to the action or the noun. The world did not collapse, the conversation didn't stop. It was just fine. She was only trying to touch and be touched, words had very little to do with it. They have very little to do with feeling, it turned out. Words have very little to do with feeling. She learned that it was all about sound really. And yet there was the poetry.

'Is it the words?'
'Of course.'
'Or the sound of it?'
'The sound.'
'Poetry must be heard, I have decided.'

30

And the shouting begins.

So you are worried about our society.

'Of course I am.'

Why?

'Because we have lost peace and civility.'

And what would you say was peace and civility?

'A face, un-defaced.'

What?

'Aman and Iman, would be indicators. Indicators of it would be when people are able to walk about outside on the streets late into the evening. Lovers walk hand in hand at night on main avenues and linger on in parks and children kick footballs in alleyways way past dark. Or when, a man lies down on the floor next to a woman and makes love to her. Aman and Iman.'

Listen, we brought you in because you agreed to do the job. We said we needed a pretty face to cover ours. Do you hear me? Pay attention! Wake up! We chose your face. You didn't really think you could do anything did you? The constitution is not for you to change. It is ours to abrogate.

'The people will protest!'

Madam the streets of this blessed country are quiet! No need for us to even impose a curfew, no need for army patrols. There are no protests. The nation sleeps. The nation rests in peace because a soldier stands guard. Do you understand? Now tell me will you cooperate? Will you be a good little girl and go on television to announce that you will behave?

There is so much pain. Only darkness now, pain overwhelms sound.

'Lie down next to me now. Here on this stone floor. Transport me, whole to that place of peace to that space, to that being of completeness of wholeness.'

'It is evening,' he says, 'wait for me

tomorrow.' She understands but she pretends not to, the look on his face is too urgent, his voice too full, her knees too weak, it is too much, and where would there be to go from there if she says she has understood? But he looks at her, indignantly, and says, 'What do you mean you don't understand? You understand everything.' And she had understood everything. And it was true, everything in his tone, in that moment, every gesture of his, had conveyed the meaning of the words that she didn't catch. The words would have been superfluous anyway. The image faded.

She sobbed, 'Wait, please wait come back! Take me with you! I will never see you again! I don't even know if you are alive, or if you are dead and if you are, if you have a grave?'

'I have a house in the mountains,' he had said.

'Yes.'

'Where I want to take you.'

'Why?'

'You should rest. Should you need to ever rest, and get away, to just rest from the world and be by yourself, then you will come there.'

'You think I will need to?' she had asked.

'There will always be a room for you.'

'I don't take up much space,' she had joked.

'Then for you I will have a small room!'

They had laughed.

'And I will lock you in,' he had smiled resolutely.

'Why?'

'I will keep the key.'

'Why?'

'So that you'll stay with me.'

'I am with you,' she had said.

'Stay.'

And she didn't know why prompted from some other place she had said, 'I don't take up too much space.' She had said this to him, who needed no persuasion.

'Then for you, I will have a very small room, and I will lock you in and keep the key, you will stay there and I will never let you go.'

'Never let me go.'

Throw her back in there, let's see how long she lasts. Throw her back in there and throw away the key!

'You will get tired of me.'

'Never.'

'You will.'

'You don't understand me.'

'You will forget, that you ever said this.'

He had looked at her with confusion. He could not understand why she was saying this. 'You will have a window from where you will see the mountains, and the snow on them, and meadows covered with flowers.'

'Flowers like the ones you bring me every day?'

'More beautiful!'

'Yes.'

'Who gives you flowers there?'

'Friends, and I buy them for myself,' she says.

'You will never need to buy flowers, you will never have to rip them from the ground, the whole world will be your vase full of flowers when you look out of your window. Will you come with me?' he asks again.

‘I cannot, we are so far apart,’ she replies.

‘What do you mean?’

‘Our circumstances,’ she says.

‘What do you mean?’

‘Don’t you know who I am?’

‘I do.’

‘Then?’

‘Then what? We are the same.’

‘How?’

‘We have nowhere to go.’

‘I have a place to go to!’ she protests.

‘Is that where you want to be?’

‘I want to be everywhere.’

‘Exactly. Going everywhere, always struggling, always alone, always controlled by someone else’s commands. We are the same,’ he says.

31

Who was she? What did she mean, do you know who I am? Who was she? When did she say this to him?

'We should be married,' he says.

'No!'

'We should have children,' he repeats.

'No.'

'Don't you want children?' he asks.

'I did want children. But for that, perhaps, it is too late now.'

'No, no, never say that,' he protests.

'Why? It's true.'

'Only God knows,' he says.

'Yes.'

'Only God will decide.'

God decided. God decided.

'Why stay when men leave anyway?' she asks.

'For the children,' he replies, simply.

Had you been the child you wanted me to have, I could have swooped you up into my arms.

'Men leave, look around you, just look here, most of the women are without their husbands, raising children on their own! These no good men. No thank you, I am fine the way I am. These no good men!'

He seemed as though she had hit him. And he had looked at her, his face had become solemn and he was silent. Then in a soft voice he had said, 'No one wants to leave their family, don't be so hard on our men. Many of our men were killed in the war. Far too many. Beautiful, brave young men.' His voice was gentle, as though he was explaining to a child. 'My brother was shot during the war and has left behind his widow and five children. That's when I returned from Moscow. I bought a gun there and I came back to fight. So don't say men leave, they don't always want to. Really, they don't always want to.'

In the darkness, she asked, 'I did apologize, didn't I? I was ashamed of myself I want to tell you that. I would not hurt you, ever. But where would I be if I had said I understood?'

32

The shouting begins.

Everybody is guilty. It's just a matter of time, before I can find out for what.

'For what?' she asks.

She's playing in the courtyard.

There's the sound of a car, a jeep, screeching to a halt.

Masked men with guns come running in.

Bandits.

They sweep her up. They fire in the air.

She screams.

Others scream too. Who are they?

They throw her into a well, those bandits, who stole her from her house.

No one will find her here.

The hole is so deep.

Her bones broke when she fell in.

She is bleeding.

It's getting dark.

She is so sad. So sad.

She'll never get a chance to grow up.

Never get a chance to see what life would be like.

Never get a chance to see.

She lives in a room, one of the rooms down the corridor.

She hears the sound of her name being called from far away. It's her mother's voice calling her in for dinner, it's a summer evening. She is playing outside. She is a sea captain, surveying the world in front of her. Wind in her hair. She rises and rises, rises up so high, so high, as high as the highest branches would take her, as high as the swing would swing her as she bent her knees and straightens out forward and backward, kneading the air, ever upward, to shout her message to her maker:

'Let me play it,

let me go,
I'll catch up with you,
when I'm done,
someday you'll have me
anyway,
then,
you can laugh at me,
or not.
But till then,
let me be,
let me show you
how I will celebrate you.
No one should,
no one can shape
my destiny for me!'
Shouting.
Talk!
'Okay.'
Will you do it?

'I would do it, I had done it. I was following the insight and advice of poetry, telling God what my will was, and it did turn out pretty much like I would have never imagined it would. Things had really turned out my way. I had two children. I had so much love. I had the house, the perfect dream house, my Mother Hubbard's cupboard, as my mother would say all the time. Or was it the old woman in the shoe? I had it. I had my parents who lived there with me, with my daughters, their nanny, the dog and the fish. The parakeets, who flew about in the house because none of us could bear cages, we could bear bird droppings, but not cages. The walls were painted the colors I felt. The living room was the yellow, the bright yellow that I had always wanted. And the entire house painted only in bright colors. It was a horror to anyone with a modicum of sobriety in their demeanor to enter our space. But in my house we had, thank God, none. We had decided to banish dullness and any inclination, whatsoever, for the understated. Our walls screamed and shouted 'Happy'. I made jams and preserves and baked bread on the weekends. We always had house guests but we made sure they came for brief periods of time. We had dinner parties almost every Friday. The rule was that Friday parties allowed us to munch on goodies from the leftovers all weekend long. The details you see, these details, these are important. You wanted details. I had it all. The family, the friends, the work, the life. Everyone said it was very brave of me, but really, I didn't understand what they were going on about. I thought I was very lucky. I thought this was the way it should be!'

Someone is shaking her, hard. There is shouting again.

What the hell is she talking about?

Sir! I think, this is it! She's gone!

Not yet. This is one tough bitch!

Please Madam! Why don't you just speak, just tell us, what we want to hear. We want to send you home, we want to go home. What are you going to get out of this?

Major! No use showing her any sympathy!

33

That night you broke us.

You broke everything.

You thieved.

You stole.

You usurped.

You kidnapped.

You thieved, you stole, you usurped, you kidnapped, us from us.

You maimed.

You sabotaged.

You raped.

You looted.

You punished.

You shot.

You whipped.

You hanged.

You executed.

You killed.

And all this time while you did all this, you managed to put on your white robes and make pilgrimages for your eternal salvation. And you made us pay.

Pay for your prayers.

Pay for your piety.

Pay for your zeal.

In my house, that night, when all was locked up, safe, concealed and the lamplight glowed upon my face and those of my sleeping family, when all was well, that night you broke in. You broke me. You dragged me out.

You punched me.

You slapped me.

You crushed me.

You smashed me.

You told me this was your house. Your house. Not mine. Not ours. Your house. Yours, yours, yours to do whatever you wanted to. Yours to decide to keep or destroy. Just yours, yours, yours!

You told me you were taking

everything, rearranging everything, breaking what you felt like breaking, trashing what didn't suit your tastes! You did not like colors, you did not like variety, you did not like too much of anything! My yellow walls, my happy, happy, house of sound, you did not like it at all!

You took away the colors.

You took away the sound.

You took away the light.

You took away my children.

You took everything, occupied everything, our bodies, our souls, our minds.

Our bodies.

Our minds.

Our souls.

Our past.

Our present.

Our future.

My children's, my parents and mine. We were not to do anything that you did not think we should. We were paralyzed, we were confined, you had imposed your law upon us.

We were not to cry.

We were not to laugh.

We were not to be angry.

We were not to be sad.

We grieved.

Yes, we grieved.

And I forgot what it meant to be angry. You destroyed my anger. It meant nothing. We did not understand what the rules were. There were none. You would decide at whim. It was all according to you, all our moves. You came in, just like that in the middle of the night, into the house that I had built, you just took over. You felt like it, so you stripped me and undid your trousers and broke into me just like you did into my house. My children Aman and Iman, my mother, you made them stand there and watch what you did, how you did it, and you made them hear me and see me scream. Because that's who you are, that's what you do. You were in control, you were absolute and they could not leave, you would not let them and when they screamed, I heard a shot. I heard a shot? What was that, what was that? In the house that I had built which you entered without permission. What was that, what is this that I remember?

Pain. Only pain.

'Who are you?

A burglar?

A thief?

A murderer?

An executioner?

An assassin?

A kidnapper?

A rapist?

A terrorist?

A mugger?

An abuser?

A psychopath?

Who are you? Who are you?'

Pain!

Sir! Hitting her won't help!

Shut up!

She keeps going. Hair swishing, dust flying, round and round. 'I'm only one in a long line of others. I'm only one, in a huge crowd.'

Flashes. Flashlights. Lenses, cameras whirring, shooting. So much light. Too much light.

'Please, I cannot see.'

'Please give her room.'

'Please shake my hand.'

'Please I cannot breathe, everyone will get a chance.'

'Everyone will get their chance.'

'Everyone wants to touch her.'

'Everyone wants a piece of history.'

'Everyone wants a piece of me.'

Madam!

'Your Excellency!'

'Please I cannot, I cannot breathe!'

I'm being pulled, hands reaching out for me. I'm being shoved. My arm feels like it's going to come out of its socket.

'Madam, one last question.'

'One last question.'

Answer my question.

'Where are my girls, where is my mother?'

Who did you think you were?

'I am.'

Did you think we would let you change the constitution?

'I have the majority.'

Get one thing straight, we are here to stay. Just tell us what we want to know. What's the use of this? What can you gain?

'You are here to go. You will go.'

Explosion, in her face. Shattering, lights.

She is gone, sir! She is gone.

Shut up!

For godssake, sir!

Shut up!

34

The sound of the dhamal rises. Drums are beating, louder and louder and louder. The world whirls all around.

Why me? Why? Who am I? Why just punch me out? Why just break a few ribs when they can rape me too. But they do that to men too. So it's not about being a man or a woman it's about being neither in their eyes. In their world it's only raw absolute power, there is nothing that withstands that. This is what they are proving to me. To me? No not to me. Only to themselves. The series of articles this week and the editorials I've been writing would do it. So maybe it has nothing to do with my being a woman. Or maybe it does. The crime, the torture, their ways, the approach that they choose has everything to do with my being a woman. They are not going to tell the world about this.

It was on a dry June morning the monsoon rains had not begun, but the skies promised their advent. Mangoes were in the peak of their season and she had had two for breakfast in her usual excessive, obsessive way. In addition, she had been drinking pitchers full of falsa juice, she remembers the colors.

Purple.

Pink.

Magenta.

White froth.

The colors of love on your body, the colors of dawn, the colors of dusk that you marked me with. Fading, fading, why did they fade away? Mangoes, yellow flesh, green skin, smooth green skin. Polished skin, reflecting light. Remember the colors. Use the black, this pitch black darkness to make these colors brighter. Use it as your backdrop. You can do it. Remember!

Remember! It is available only for a short time, overdose on it. Eat those mangoes till you are sick of them, till you have had enough. Only I never had enough of you. I never had enough of you!

The sunlight wanes, castes a glow on their bodies. They lie on their sides facing each other holding each other in an embrace. It comes so easily to him, to hold her in this way. And suddenly he asked her, 'How do you love me?' She is perplexed. She doesn't know what to say. She doesn't have the language but she doesn't have the desire for guile either. She is glad for the lack of words. No poetry. No eloquence. He has asked her simply and she has no answer.

'How do you love me?'

He has told her in a thousand different ways, with kisses and words. A thousand different ways with your eyes, your words, your touch.

'How do I love you?'

She strokes his face, kisses his eyes, but he won't be satisfied.

'How?' he asks.

'I don't have words.'

She doesn't know how to say the word 'more'. She can say, 'than life'.

In the darkness she says out loud, 'I will write to you, I write to tell you. How? This must reach you. Someone will get this to you. This is my will. Have this translated and make sure it reaches him.'

'You asked me how I loved you. How do you love me? And I had been left without words. I didn't want to say something poetic and eloquent. I wanted to be truthful. How do I love you? I love you just like this. With my body and what it has to offer. I give you this. I love you. You are the one true thing in my life. I love you, like I love truth. I love you like I love God. I love you like I love water.'

'Like water?'

'Yes like water. You are water to me. Life and drowning. I love you. Water, like rain, like water from deep within the earth, sweet, clean, cold, like snow, like clouds, like sky, like the sweet sweat on your body, like my tears. I love you like that. Like water, like the color of your eyes, I love you like that. I love you like water, that's how.'

To be with the color of your eyes, the color of parched mountain grass in a rainless summer. To be with your skin, to be washed by sun and wind and to be with you, your child-like self. How easy it would have been to have just vanished with you. How easy it would have been to have melted into the mountains, the sun, the wind. How easy would it have been to have left everything forever, the city, Jack, this life, that life, all of it. How easy? But no, I wasn't there to stay, wasn't there to live. I had a gift in mind to take from you, you were my chosen one, to love and to leave and to carry with me forever.

She flies away. Further and further away, rising higher and higher up into the sky above the fields, the rivers, the mountains. His mountains. She hopes and she prays that she carries a child with her, made of all the love they had made.

I think of you, only you. Only you, only you, only you. Your poetry, your song, your laughter, your dancing, your funny words, your own language. I think of that as being you.

Not the story that was printed.

Not the edited story.

Not the story that got me noticed.

Not the one that brought them to my door.

Not the one that made me a hero.

Not the one that made me valuable for them.

Not the one that brought this.

Not the one that brought all of this.

But the one that will see me through. That one, that one.

Without words.

That one in the language without words.

Your light remains my story, your shimmer, that blinds the grief. The grief, of pain that you have seen, the sorrow your eyes have seen: war, death, sickness, pain, hunger and cold. And yet you have not become that. Only my story has. The one that won the prize, the one that got me recognized. You are passion. See, I know how to find phrases for it. I cannot feel it, I cannot be it. I am an observer, I was there to write a story. And all your ferocious wanting, your passion, your gestures, your gentleness cannot put me back inside of me. I am, where I am not.

When I awaken as light comes in at dawn, I see my body in your arms, you are holding me close against you, my cheek wet against your moist chest. I see this. Your scent is sweet. I know this, I think of words for it. I lie that way, thinking of your sweetness, you do not have any other smell. Your whole being is sweet. Your name is sweet. Your sounds are sweet. Surely, I will be forgiven for this? Surely God will be kind, God will be kind. He must come. There is so little time.

She can feel him, she can feel his presence.

She senses it.

She always has.

Don't forget my words, don't forget what I have said to you. He says this to her. She wants to reply. Still unable to say how much.

Then the noise.

Sooner or later you will speak!

What is it that they want to know? I haven't done anything wrong. He and I had pronounced each other man and wife, I am his wife and he is my husband. God watched that. He was our witness.

'I am married to you.'

'I to you,' he completes her.

And that is all.

'We are our witnesses.'

And God is our witness. Why should there be anyone else? It is our will, in His presence. Can it be any other way? Did He not will this? Can that be so?

'Is that what you want to know. Is that what you want me to speak about?'

What is she going on about? Who is she talking about?

Sir, I think we won't get anymore.

'How dare you punish me!'

Did you hear that? What did she say? The bitch still has some juice left!

'How dare you punish me? Yes, it was my decision! All mine! Is that what you want from me? Is that what you want me to confess about?'

What is she going on about?

Pain.

Sir, she's an old lady, for godssake!

She hears someone pleading. Is it him? It gives her strength. 'My decision, do you hear me. I will be alone in it. You cannot scare me, I am not frightened of you. I am so far ahead of you, I have already stepped far into the road. We shall see what this route brings. Do you know how I hoped? Do you know the meaning of hope? Do you know how I prayed? Do you know the meaning of prayer? I prayed, for the good news. Yes, I would be a mother. And that was to be and I was ready. I bore my children for the sake of that privilege and bore all that it brought upon me.'

Sir, please, let her go, cut her down, she is only babbling!

I don't think so!

She is gone. Hurting her more than this won't help.

'How dare you punish me!' she continues to struggle.

Pain.

Stop it! Stop it!

'First, I will be judged as a sinner, and then as a mother. I sinned to love. I love him. I sinned to be a mother. How wrong is that? I will ask God am I a sinner or a life lived. To be.'

And she was chosen to be.
To be.
To not bargain,
to not negotiate,
to not weigh her options,
to not choose with her mind,
to choose with her heart.
To only feel.
To be lost,
to be completely lost.
To be lost,
to be found,
to drown,
to drink,
to drown.
I love you.
I love you like water.

To lose over and over again, and still choose to risk again and again, to plunge deeply, to gain what she would have nothing to show for. To be rich, to be wealthy in love. To never settle for less.

'No, not I. I chose, I loved, I gave of myself completely. I loved completely. I lost completely. I was never sparing of anything, my words, my movements, or my emotions, never sparing in my action. And now I'm paying for it. How long has it been? A night, several hours, days? I do not know. It must be at least six hours because now I am hungry and I always get hungry after three hours. I am so hungry. I want chapli kebabs and naan. When I get out of here when my mother, Aman and Iman come to get me, the first thing we are going to do is to go and get chapli kebabs on the way home. And really piping hot naan. Fresh naan from the tandoor. I'll probably eat it all in the car even before we get home and Aman and Iman will shriek with mirth to watch their mamma eat like that, like she'll never see food again. See food again.

'Sea Food!' Aman shouts at me gleefully, in the fish restaurant and opens her mouth wide to show me the glob of masticated rahu in her mouth.

'Sea Food-See food, Mamma, see?'

35

'Stay with me,' he says to her.

'I cannot,' she replies. 'You know, you love me for what I am. And I am this. I leave.'

'Is this you? Or is it your work?'

'Work.'

'You can work here. Everyone works here.'

'Yes. But you know what I do.'

'I work too.'

She laughs, 'Fighting wars, isn't work. At least not what I consider work.'

'Why not? What about the military?'

'You aren't in the military.'

'Not a state sanctioned one. But God's military!'

'Okay, see, that's where it starts to get crazy.'

'I don't want to argue with you either. But as far as I know and what I see, your work is like my work, I work like you do.'

'I would disagree,' she says.

'Why? We are the same, I go where the battle takes me, you go where the stories are. I have a weapon and so do you. I sleep in tents, under the sky, in trucks or in barracks and you in hotels. Neither of us has a house of our own. So how are we different?'

The darkness. There is a garden, that garden of two fountains. I am seated on the bench near the center surrounded by pine trees watching the pigeons flutter about in the fountain in front of me. Listening to the sound of water, the sound of pigeons cooing, the flutter of wings, other birds twittering and chirping, and chattering, tweet, tweet, tweeting, the fragrant air of apple blossoms and pine-cones and pine-needles. Dappled sunlight coming through the leaves. This is the most perfect of places. I feel as though I am in a place in heaven.

'Was it too much to have asked for?'

What is she talking about?

'Have I been too greedy?'

Here it comes, she's beginning to sing! Everyone does!

'Have I been too self-centered, too selfish all my life that to have asked for love would have been too much?'

What the hell?

'What was it that I was expecting, looking for, waiting for? To be able to see the face of God, to be near that feeling, to be near death to be alive, to be everything in that one ultimate experience. Was that far too much?'

What?

36

Humza lights a cigarette. His hands are shaking. He searches the face of Colonel Zafar Riaz. 'I don't think she'll break.'

Colonel Riaz is leaning against a verandah pillar, smoking pensively, staring at Humza, he doesn't seem to notice the hot sun or the heat. 'It's a matter of time, she'll break, they all do.'

'She doesn't even seem to know what we're talking about.'

'Don't get confused my friend, she knows. She thinks she can play the victim with us. This is politics. She's a politician. She thinks she is gaining time and that someone is bound to raise a protest and she'll be saved. That all her cronies all over the world will come swooping down on us with sanctions, protests and boycotts! That's the difference between people like her and people like us.'

'What difference?'

'Those who look to the outside always and those whose strength is within. The difference between politicians versus heroes.'

'Which ones are we?' Humza asks coldly.

Colonel Riaz gazes back at him, curls his lips back in a pucker and blows out smoke. His eyes are cold. Blue-green cold. 'I admire you, you're one of our finest,' he says lazily.

Humza tenses, looks away towards the parade grounds. The afternoon white light is blinding. He can't see very far, the light hurts his eyes, they begin to tear.

'But twenty years since the academy and I'm still a major!'

'Be patient, my friend!' the Colonel laughs.

'Snow one day, sand the next. Hero one day, a jailer of women the next.'

'We can always send you back up again!'

'Martyrdom?'

'Well that's what you seem to want,' Colonel Riaz laughs.

Humza forces himself to chuckle, then draws deeply on his cigarette and looks away towards the parade ground and sees another place.

Sun rises.

A flutter.

Light on water.

Bird takes wing.

Then another.

37

Open this damn door! Steel for godssake! Is this necessary? Does anyone think she can go anywhere? Oh for godssake!

Sir!

Just look at her! Do it, Fareed! I said inject her, for the love of God, she's a mess.

I don't know how to.

Give me the injection, I'll do it.

We'll be court martialed for this!

We can only pray for that!

The beauty of the hunt at dawn.

The perfect ethics of a clean shoot.

Painless. To kill without causing pain.

Ethical.

Moral.

A duty.

An obligation.

A noble thing.

A commitment.

A burden.

Humza steps out. Colonel Riaz is waiting for him, blocking his path. Humza brushes past him down the corridor.

'Major!' Colonel Riaz thunders, his voice cracking with the force of his anger. 'Major Jahanzeb come back here, this minute!'

Humza stops. Turns around, walks back, the sound of his boots tap out the silence around them. He hasn't noticed the sound of his boots before. This is what silence is. He stares at the fury that is the Colonel's face.

'Major Jahanzeb, Major Humza Jahanzeb, I am going to have you arrested!'

'Really, Colonel? For what?' Humza moves closer to the man.

'For insubordination! For disobeying orders! Orders of your superiors! Aiding and abetting a traitor! In short you are about to face charges of high treason and you will be, I promise you that, you will be court martialed. I promise you that!'

Humza turns, and walks away. The sound of his boots please him.

'Major! Did you hear me! Major!'

Humza stops. Another chance to walk back. He does. He comes closer to the Colonel. Their bodies almost touch. Humza's face is very close to the Colonel's face. Almost kissing distance away from the Colonel's mouth. Humza clenches his teeth and in a tone he knows the Colonel will understand, will not mistake, a tone that the Colonel would himself have used just before a killing, he says, 'Don't ever try to threaten me again, Colonel. I'll do what I think is right. I'll say this to you just once, just once. If you ever bring this up again, I'll kill you. See these hands, these bare hands will finish you. Don't ever threaten me again. Don't you dare ever talk patriotism to me. Don't ever talk to me about courage. Don't ever pull that on me. I'll kill you. Try touching me, you spying son of a bitch. Just try. I'll pull your heart out with my bare hands and feed it to the dogs. Insubordination? Insubordination?

Fuck you! You can't touch me, you don't deserve to be in the same space as me. I'm the grandson of a general, I'm the son of a general, I'm the nephew of generals, brigadiers, colonels, and the brother, cousin and friend of generals, brigadiers, colonels, majors, lieutenants and captains. Every staff college in this country, every academy, every barrack, every cantonment carries the photographs and the stories of the legends that I come from. Come to my village some day, and I'll show you heroism and valor, weighed by the tons in brass that we carry on our chests for patriotism and heroism. I am the nephew of four uncles who were killed in the line of duty. You bloody upstart, bloodthirsty, ambitious, scheming, mother fucking, son of a bitch! Get out of my sight! Now!' Humza waits.

Colonel Riaz does as he is told.

The beauty of the hunt at dawn.

The perfect ethics of a clean shoot.

Painless. To kill without causing pain.

Ethical.

Moral.

A duty.

An obligation.

A noble thing.

A commitment.

A burden.

I have to go now. I'll come again.

'Stay,' she says.

I cannot.

'Let me go then.'

I cannot.

'Why not?'

I have orders to respect.

'I know. But you will not.'

Why not?

'Against my will?'

He whispers now.

No.

He moves towards her and injects her in her arm.

This will make you feel better.

'Thank you,' she says.

It's all I can do. You see I am a hero.

38

Time. To live it all now, in this limited time. To stretch this and make it all there is. In which we will not be affected by all that lies ahead and outside this enchanted feeling between us. In which we are untouched and unaffected, unharmed and undamaged by the ravages of the world outside of us: age, language, distance, everything, everything. I love you like water. Like water, like a flood, you drown me. There is nothing else, only this, only this. In every possible way this is impossible and yet in every possible way this is what should be, this is all there is. And as I teeter on the brink of decision on the brink of plunging, it can either be the edge of a precipice or it can be an inexplicable freedom of being, just being. To live in this moment and not worry, to not be afraid of the past or the future.

Where are you now?

Where are you since I left? Are you happy?

Are you as I wanted you to be?

She imagines him unbraiding the hair of his bride, hundreds of thin braids down to her ankle. It would take him at least half the night as his bride would sit beside him, trembling, for him to slowly and carefully and gently, so as not to hurt her, undo each braid. And as he would unbraid her hair, she would tell him stories, of her childhood, her dreams, her worries, her concerns, what would make her happy. Each strand of hair loosened would make her more relaxed, he would feel her shoulders begin to relax, her face soften, as though as he unbraided, he unbound her, freed her, made her speak without concern.

She has his smile, he understands each word she says. She understands his words completely. And he listens and unbraids, and he thinks of someone else. He thinks of her. So long ago, that woman who understood only his touch, the language of his touch. His bride looks up at him, shyly and with trust, and he smiles back at her with kindness and love. He strokes her head, her neck, and she bends towards him. And all else is forgotten, all there is, is that which is lived.

Time is running out. But maybe the story will live on and stay young, go on loving, living, laughing, dancing, exchanging glances, touching hands. She struggles to remain in that moment when everything was simple.

'Should have said yes and walked with you. But know this, Aman and Iman are on their way to you. My mother will find you. She has the address. I know she will find you. Take care of your children, you will see me in their faces, they have your eyes, and your ability to be friends with everyone. And they have my impulsiveness. You will instantly recognize us. I told you I couldn't have children and you said, trust in God. He would decide. It was not up to me, you had warned me, it was up to God. God decided. He decided. We may have sinned. But the children are innocent, born of love. And God will protect them, and you. God bless the three of you. Aman, Iman and you.'

She thinks she has children?

Pain.

That moment in which I was, that moment of just being, just being without a context. That moment before time, place, circumstances, need. Things spoil everything. Facts, instead of feelings. Force instead of freedom.

'You unbind me. With you, I am free.'

39

Water.

God, You have always met me, in your appointed places. Here we are again, at this spring of clear water, at this pond of clarity, luminous fish, the sound of a gurgling spring rushing up from the center of the earth. And I am asking You: tell me what to do, what next, what have You planned for me, and in the water I see Your creation reflected back, it says the pond is like your heart, what you have in your heart is My will.

Remember. Don't think so much you had said, don't look for so much meaning.

There is only this, there is only love. It is simple, it is clear. Integrity. 'You don't believe?' you had asked me. For I had too many explanations. I am lying here today, because they are saying the same thing. I think that I have written something. About us? And they think I have blasphemed. I think they are going to kill me. I think that's what it is. Why didn't I stay with you? I must remember. The state into which the whole world disappeared and folded. Those waves and waves that made all time and distance disappear. That height reached, those steps climbed. Feel it, feel, it. Your mouth stops my words, 'Don't blaspheme, don't blaspheme.'

He has not punished me. He gave me you and then the children. I lived with them and I brought them up. They are set in their ways. And now God gave me this. And this, this broken face, and smashed body, this is the work of men. This is the will of men. God's will has been done, and this, I will wait to find out what this is.

She is falling, without end. There is pain without mitigation. How is she to stop it? How is she to end this? What's to focus on, where should she place herself? Only darkness now. But she must struggle against it. Escape it. Be in another place. There is a large table, almost as large as a kitchen table, rough surface. On it is a large jar with wild flowers, long stalks of yellow flowers. Around the table, there are wooden chairs, the table is covered with paper, books, pencils. There are large windows all around. There is no other furniture in the room. A colorful rug, a large soft cloth mattress for them to lie on and cushions against the wall. On the table dried fruit, walnuts, raisins, almonds, apricots, and figs. And at the table she is seated and he appears. This is where he will be.

A fire burning, heat rising slowly, a warmth, a glow from your skin into mine. We know. A knowledge, deeper each day. And every single day, I the jaded one, the cynic, think you are done. The mystery is over and each day, you humble me. There is no mystery, it is clear. And each day, each time we are lying back in each others arms, you ask me to stay, each day, each morning.

'Stay.'

'No.'

'You know this is wrong. We are sinning.'

'Does this feel wrong?'

You shake your head. And you cover my mouth with your fingers, 'Don't say such things,' you say. I kiss your fingers and you remove them from my mouth. You place your mouth on mine and kiss me and bite my lips till I think they will bleed.

Tell me that I will see you again. Tell me that when I wake from this sleep that I am being pulled towards, that when I awaken you will be here. That I will awaken to the knock on the door, that my heart will be beating so hard, and that it will be you, standing there, when I open the door, and you will smile and laugh and I will jump with joy and we will begin all over again. And you will whisper, is everything alright? And I'll nod and say yes.

And so, if it is, His will that be done. And it is. Done. And love and living is and will be. And sin, is to sin against the loved one.

'Accept me as I am,' he says.

'I do,' she replies.

'No. Just accept,' he insists.

'There is no more time left,' she says.

'How can you say that?' he protests.

'Love, I feel it,' she says.

'How?' he asks.

'I am slipping,' she replies.

I will not let you.

'You cannot help me.'

That is the greatest sorrow, that you will not let me.

The greatest sorrow.

I am slipping.

I will not let you.

You cannot help me.

She slips away.

40

Before this, she had searched for a way out. She had done this before. Then, that time, before this, she had found a way to escape. From him. To escape from his love and from his devotion. To escape, having to stay.

'You must know. I must tell you. I am here to get a story. That's all. There is a man, a good trusting man, waiting for me, when I go home.' There was no other way to leave.

He stands there in front of her. Trying to understand. He understands the meaning of her sentences by the way she speaks them. Her tone.

He says, 'I can tell by your eyes.' And when he finally understands, he slaps her and grabs her throat, and looks straight into her eyes. She looks back into his, she thinks he is going to squeeze but he doesn't, he lets go, and steps back. His eyes are full of rage. She looks straight into them. And he looks straight back into hers. His eyes hold hers while his hand reaches for his waist. His hand reaches and draws a knife from a sheath in his belt. She stands very still. She sees the knife. She sees the knife move, she sees it in his hand, she sees his hand move through the air. She sees it, the knife, catch the light, the motion is so quick, and he has moved so swiftly, she marvels at his grace, she marvels at his calmness, she marvels at herself. And she has shut her eyes. And through her shut eyes, she sees again, the hand in motion, the knife catch the light, and she waits.

She sees herself waiting.

A second, only a second, maybe less.

She hears him cry out. Blood spurts up at her.

There is blood and she feels its warmth.

She opens her eyes, to look at herself. She is splattered with blood. But she doesn't feel the pain. She looks towards where the knife is.

It is on him. He has slashed his arm, he has cut a piece of flesh off his arm. He holds a piece of his own flesh, with his thumb against the knife. The pain hits her.

She opens her mouth to scream, but nothing happens. There is no sound. He hasn't moved his gaze off her. Her wide open eyes stare in terror at the bleeding white, pink, red piece of his flesh, that he holds, between the knife and his thumb. He throws his flesh at her. He throws it at her. She flinches, her face shielded by her arms. Blood all over.

He throws himself at her. She leans into him, he into her, but he will not embrace her. He is sobbing. He speaks in agony through clenched teeth.

'I am not the person you make me out to be.'

She sinks.

He leaves.

She will never see him again.

'Heal me. Tell me that you will,

beyond the ceremony of sanctioning, love me. Without the sanctimony, when time no longer will be kind to me, when life itself will begin to recede from me. Then. Will you be there for me? Will you have space for me? Poems for me? Will you lift me up in your arms and dance around the room with me? Tell me. Heal me. Tell me that if I were weak and sick and poor and unable to care for myself, you would be my strength, my wealth, my will. Tell me. Heal me. Tell me that you see me. And not some illusion of something you dream of. Tell me. Heal me.'

41

She hears footsteps in the distance. Boots on a cement floor, the sound echoes in the corridor. They are coming for her again.

There is nothing left for them to come for.

She smells the scent of *Fidji.*

We'll be home soon.

Will I be asleep?

Yes.

She doesn't understand, what it is that they want her to tell them.

She would gladly tell them everything that they want to know. Only, what is it? Who are they? Who is she?

But, now, there is no time left. And, she is determined not to go this way. To go back, to go back to that one perfect moment. It is quite simple, in the end, really. At the end what is left? What is it that's left to think about at this moment, in these last few moments of breath, caught, precariously, between pain and painlessness? She understood it, and there it was. Just there, over there, nearly there. There. There, in the house, in the mountains. There, in the room with the window. There, where she was at the window, gazing out at the meadow. She turns away from the window and walks out of the room into the corridor. A cool, dry, still afternoon. Silent, no one is in the house. Everyone must be working in the orchards or the fields. She looks around her and thinks about returning to her room, but she feels that she cannot be wrong, she knows that he will come here, he knows she is here. She knows by now that he knows that she will be waiting for him.

The helicopter will arrive tomorrow. It will land on the meadow and lift her up. He must come. There is so little time. She can feel him, she can feel his presence. She senses it. She always has. And so she has returned, here, in the afternoon, though she should not be here, there are still at least four more hours in the day and she could be meeting with people. She has made an excuse that she is tired. She has told them she is done for the day. She stands in the tiny corridor, and then the door, several doors down the corridor, opens and he steps out as though this were planned. He strides down the length of the distance between them, swiftly, and as he comes down the corridor towards her she looks at him solemnly, almost in a panic. She tries to, but cannot manage a smile and neither does he. As she enters her room, her hand still on the door, he covers it with his hand and he enters. He waits, looking straight into her eyes.

She shuts the door. She shuts the door on all the doubts and misgivings. That world where everything is analyzed and weighed carefully before a move is made, the place of being above it all, recedes, she has shut it all out. All of it, she has shut the door on it, because this, this cannot be ignored, this must not be rejected, this is where all of her existence culminates, this is the crescendo, this is the majesty of all existence.

The room is dark, the curtains are drawn, it takes a moment for their eyes to adjust. She can feel the blood rushing through her down into her legs. Her legs hurt her, she can hardly stand. She identifies this as fear. She tells herself that it is fear. The fear of being alive. But she doesn't care. She is in a different place now. There is just him and there is her. There is a thrill beginning. She is again as though, waiting at the foot of the lawn, a little girl, she can see the storm gathering on the plains, in the distance there is Mardan, it's already raining in Mardan. She can see the sheets of rain from the sky to the earth there, over there, beyond the river beyond the plains. The Indus is in full flood. She watches from her vantage point on the lawn on the hilltop as the dust cloud begins to come closer. She waits, she calculates, she controls the fear that is rising in her. Both her hands hold on to the dog's leather collar, he is barking and beginning to whine, the wind is rising and his white fur is blowing back, her hair is all over her face, but she waits until the cloud of dust reaches nearer the shore of the river on the other side and then she can't hold on any longer. He is straining and trying to free himself from her, she lets go of the collar and he bolts towards the house and she turns and runs as fast as she can in his wake, leaping up the steps two at time to the second lawn and then to the first, she can feel the fat plops of rain drops on her bare arms just as she clears the first lawn and climbs the steps to the front verandah of the house. The storm hits, there's lightning and the air all around darkens and thickens with dust, the wind is blowing hard now, the dog is howling and barking and she is shrieking with excitement. She has reached the verandah, before the storm caught her, she has reached safety, she did it! She did it! She did it! She looks around her, she is her witness, only she, the dog and the storm. Clouds continue to thunder, the storm thickens with dust. Thick and sweet with the smell of wet dust, how sweet this darkness, how sweet the sound of the storm, the sweet smell and sound of darkness.

They stand close, she is breathing hard as though she has been running, her heart is beating fast and she can feel its pulse throbbing in her neck. He steps back facing her and leans against the wall, he is breathing hard, unevenly. She steps back too and leans against the wall opposite him, they are in the narrow corridor leading into her room. She moves her arm forward towards his face, intending to touch him, to caress the skin on his cheek-bone, the lines near his eyes, but she miscalculates the distance, there's too much between them, but he is there crossing it, that distance between them, and before she can move, he has crossed over and she is in his arms.

Their arms are around each other, they hold each other around the waist, their palms moving upwards towards each other's shoulder blades, pushing them, moving them into each other. She moves her fingers down his spine, one vertebra at a time, feeling him tremble against her, then he is very still, very still, and he follows her lead. She imagines a light, a golden light filling the spaces between each section of her spine. The golden light fills her with warmth, makes her shine. She is growing longer and longer, it's rushing up and down and up through the tip of her head. Surely, she must be glowing, the entire room must be glowing. Yes, there is light, her eyes are shut but there is so much light.

She hears inside of her head the words, cervical, lumbar, thoracic, sacrum. Nothing has sounded so beautiful, what beauty these words have, cervical, lumbar, thoracic, sacrum. Sacrum, sacrum. Where is that? It's the spine, she knows, but which part of it, where?

Her legs won't hold her but he holds her weight against him. She wants to rise up so that they fit into each other. But he bends at the knee and readjusts her and she feels as though she has been lifted up, as though she has grown taller, that her spine has stretched.

She is aware that there is complete silence and yet the sound between them is like that of the helicopter landing, like the storm from across the river, crashing at her heels, and she cannot control it, it cannot be contained here, in this room, but it must, will it remain within their bodies? She can hear him clearly, she can hear him clearly, yet he has not spoken there have been no words. And yet. And the aching has now turned into a light, it glows, its heat is giving her sight. She leans against him, her back is against the cool wall. And slowly she is slipping towards the floor. He steadies her, he props her up against the wall with both his hands against her shoulders, he slides down. Here, right here, yes, she thinks. She cannot take any chances. This moment, she cannot risk losing it, she cannot let it change. He is on his knees, his face is buried against her stomach, he holds her around the waist. She strokes his head, his cheek rests against her stomach. She jerks, involuntarily as she feels his tongue licking her navel. He looks up at her uncertainly, his eyes are wide, inquiring, his hand moves up her body, over her breasts up to her face, his fingers are in her mouth. His tongue traces a line downwards and on to her thighs, she thinks she's going to faint. She slips onto the floor and takes him down with her. She sees the helicopter landing tomorrow. It's strange that she should think ahead to afterwards. There is nothing after this.

He is above her, propped up on his elbows, pushing her hair away from her face, smoothening out her hair again and again, his fingers are caught in her hair, tangling it, he kisses her forehead, her eyes, her temples, the palm of her hand that has reached up to his face. And then he turns her, half over, and kisses her shoulder blades and bites her taking a large chunk of her flesh between his lips, his teeth are pressed into her flesh, just enough. She wants him to leave a mark, she must have memory of this, there must be something, she hopes he'll draw blood. He draws back to inspect the bruise on her skin, and then he kisses her harder biting her with his lips and teeth, on her neck, then draws back to see the blue begin, then her shoulders, then her arms. She is struggling to keep that world out of her thoughts. She looks up and back at his face, his mouth covers hers, and she moves back, her back is against the floor again, and suddenly, she is uncertain, but he grabs her shoulder and presses it down, he kisses her on her shoulder near where her hand is. Her arms embrace him. He unwinds her arms from around him and moves them above her head, their fingers entwine and their palms are pressed into each other. She presses harder, she wants to feel the lines in his hands against hers. She want this, she wants this. The lines on her palms must feel, they are aching with desire. She doesn't know how he senses it and he rakes his fingernails over her palm, she moans and their fingers clasp each other again. He kisses her face and then his tongue finds hers, pushes it back as it enters her mouth, he kisses her. It's as though he is licking her mouth with his tongue and his lips as though they were some sort of succulent fruit, like a plum, too ripe too juicy to be had any other way, and she can see an image of a woman sucking at a fruit, she saw her in the bazaar yesterday.

He bites her on her arms and on her stomach and on her breasts. And she is not sure whether she is in pain or in pleasure she is not sure, whether she wants to protest, or plead for him to continue.

His hand struggles with hers and her arm is stretched back, against his, above her head and he takes a few gentle nips, one, two, and three on the right, and one, two and three on the left and then a hard bite again, just to be fair. And as her hand tries to free itself he quickly moves back upwards to her throat, his mouth is against the side of her neck just below the ear and he is blowing on her neck, his lips are pressed gently against her skin and she thinks his lips seem to have found fruit again and his mouth and tongue are licking the length of her neck. She struggles to free her arms, and she is moaning and it's aloud. He tries to caution her, so his mouth moves over hers and once she's understood, then he goes back to the fruit that he has found, and then he knows, he knows as her hips rise under him, off the floor, his arm moves down under her back, his palm finds the arch of her back and supports her and moves down to her hips.

His face is so serious, so tender, so intent, she is all that there is, she is all that exists in his eyes and then his hips lunge forward into her and they are moving together. And she is crying and his tongue is licking up the tears and he is whispering, 'Why?' and he is shushing her and she is beginning to laugh and he laughs and then they are locked in their waves, their rhythms and the waves are rising and they are on them and they are balancing on them higher and higher further up, and each wave stretches and stretches and now there is no further to go. And when they can't stretch anymore and they've reached as far into themselves and out towards each other as they can, and down into each other and into themselves as far and as deep as it is possible, they let go and rush down the slopes, the crests of the wave, here they go and here they come and here they come, oh God! Here is Truth. Truth. Here it is in these waves, in these peaks in these valleys in this bright light in this oblivion, in this sound. Beloved.

I see you in the meadows.

I see you in the snow and you are motioning to me to follow.

I fall into the luscious light, languid shadows, lazy sleep, lying beneath your milky warmth, dreaming love.

We'll be home soon.

Will I be asleep?

Yes.